M
Art Gallery

A Mandy and Roger Cozy Mystery

Book 1

Eleanor Kittering

This book is a work of fiction. All situations, characters and dialogues are part of the author's imagination. Although real locations may be referred to, they have no relation to any persons, living or dead and any resemblance is entirely coincidental. .

CONTENTS

To Get A Free Audiobook Version of this Book

Go to:

http://audiobooksignup.higher-understanding.com

PROLOGUE

Roger Fahey's shift was coming to an end. It was nearing four o'clock and he was looking forward to having a drink and studying his prospects for the evening. As a New York City detective, he welcomed all the positives of life. The war had ended a year ago, and so far, 1947 was shaping up to be great, with endless possibilities. As he left the building, he spotted his coworker, and fellow detective- Joe Gaynor.

"So Roger, are you finally going to ask that waitress out? If you keep eating at that place just to see her, you're going to get fat." Joe laughed.

"Listen Joe, she's a nice girl and I don't want to rush this. I want her to get to know me as a normal person, not a cop, and I'd like to find out more about her. I'm gonna ask her out tonight, so don't worry about me losing my boyish figure."

"Yeah, but she already knows you're a cop."

"Yes, and she's still interested in me. A lot of other women would have run away. I think things are going swell. I'll see you tomorrow."

"See you tomorrow Roger, good luck."

Roger relished his first whiff of fresh air as he stepped out of the station. He thought of going to the restaurant to ask Rosalie out; would she like to go to a movie? Or maybe go to a show? He was thinking about maybe getting a new apartment.

He was so caught up in his thoughts as he crossed the street, that he didn't see the car that hurtled towards him. In no time at all Roger and the car made contact. The car sped away. Roger lied dead in the street- a crumpled heap of broken bones and internal organs.

He stood at the side of the street. For a moment, he had the urge to chase the car. He stared at it until it became a distant dot on the horizon. He could also see his body. Just laying there on the street in a very awkward position. What he was staring at was his own corpse.

There was a man who stood to Roger's left. The man stared at Roger's corpse and shook his head as if to say: 'What a shame.'

Upon seeing him, Roger asked "Who are you?"

"Oh hi, sorry for not speaking up sooner, you were engaged in thinking that maybe you would chase the car. My name is Colin and I'm your guardian angel."

"What?"

"Well Roger, as you may have surmised by now, this was a pre-meditated hit by the mob, since you have refused to go on the take for them. They decided to rub you out."

Roger looked at Colin a little confused.

"You mean, I'm dead?"

"I'm sorry to say, yes Roger. That's why you're looking at your dead body. And I'm here to take you to the next level."

By now a crowd had gathered and officers from the station had come to oversee the process. Joe was there, sad to learn that Roger was the victim of the "accident". Joe had been one of the first to respond when somebody came in the station and said 'somebody got run over, I think it's a cop'.

"This is nuts. Look at all these people." Roger said.

"Roger, they're here to take your body to the morgue. See Joe over there? He doesn't look too happy cause he knows what happened to you."

Roger went over to Joe.

"Joe, it's me Roger, I'm still here!"

"I'm afraid he can't hear you Roger. You're now a spirit."

Roger watched the paramedics load his body into an ambulance.

"But isn't there a way for me to get back? I feel fine."

"Yes Roger, your spirit feels fine, however, your body has ceased to be a vessel that you can utilize to live your earthly life."

"I can't believe that this has happened to me. And here I was planning to ask Rosalie out and maybe get a new apartment. This really stinks."

"Sorry Roger, I'm afraid Rosalie is going to be heartbroken."

"Me too. You know, she was the first dame I've met after my first wife that I actually clicked with. I've grown up a lot since my first marriage, I really thought that this was going to be a go."

"Roger, your life had marvelous possibilities. Unfortunately, in your occupation, as an honest cop, you fell afoul of organized crime. You were a liability and they decided to eliminate you."

"That's those weasels for you, they'll never face you man to man, always behind your back or from a car."

"It's ok Roger, no need to get more upset than you already are. Come, there's nothing for us to here, it's your colleague's job now to clean up this mess. We have to go to the waiting station."

"The waiting station?"

"I'll explain as we go along."

Before he could take his last look at the world as he knew it, Roger was transported to a strange, white corridor. White was everywhere, save the windows along the corridor, through which Roger could see beautiful gardens.

"Welcome to the waiting station"

"This is it?"

"Well, this is the main reception area, Roger. There are grounds, as you can see from the windows, and places of occupation for the different inhabitants."

"Of which I am now one, I gather?"

"For a while anyway. We have to plan the next stage of your spiritual evolution."

"My spiritual evolution?"

"Roger you don't have to repeat everything I say, as a question."

"Oh, that's easy for you to say. Listen, just twenty minutes ago, I was planning on asking Rosalie out, thinking that life wasn't so bad after all. Now I'm with you, what was your name again?"

"Colin"

"Right. Colin. Sorry. Well, now I'm with you in some kind of station, waiting for who-knows-what, and you're talking evolution like I'm a monkey or something?"

"Roger, I perfectly understand being upset, it happens to everybody who experiences a sudden death like you did. There was no preparation, you didn't see it coming. And all of a sudden, you're with your guardian angel in a strange environment."

"Ok, tell me this, if you're my guardian angel, why didn't you protect me from getting run over?"

"Because Roger, if this attempt failed, there would have been another attempt in the near future. And we would be in exactly the same place we are now. You see, you didn't want to be on the take from the mob. On the other hand, look at Joe. They made him an offer, either go on the take, stop being a cop or die. That's why he's going to work for his cousin Willy. You know how he told you that there's more money in the dry cleaning business? That was just a ruse."

"So, why didn't they make me an offer?"

"Because they know you Roger, you would have gotten all high and mighty with them, that you were anti-corruption, how you were going to take them down single-handedly, there would have been NO negotiating with you. Which is an admirable quality, I must say, but a death sentence in your case."

"Yeah, you're right, I just hate those guys."

"And they hate you. New York has always been a corrupt town. Thirteen years of prohibition and the war didn't help one bit. Organized crime just grew and grew. Now, it's a way of life for a lot of people."

"You're right, they would have bumped me off next week or over the weekend, at their earliest convenience."

"Well, don't dwell on that anymore Roger, I'll get you a drink."

"You can drink here?"

"We're in the waiting station Roger. You are being transitioned and even though you really don't need to eat or drink, it's what you're used to. It's all relative."

"You know Colin, every time I think you're going to

make things clearer, I just get more confused."

"Well, maybe a drink will help." Colin smiled as he walked away. He returned within two seconds, a glass in hand. "Here, drink this."

Roger gripped the glass and took a long drink. "Hey this is good, what is it?"

"I believe in your world, it's called a zombie."

Roger made a face "Very funny, I got a guardian angel who's a comedian."

"Just having a little joke. But now to more serious matters. Most people that wind up here, Roger don't have options. They go directly to what we call the netherworld. It is a place where those whose lives have been cut short can live out the rest of their allotted time. They, however, haven't led exemplary lives."

"Wait, I can see where this is going. I haven't led an exemplary life, so I'm going to the netherworld, right?"

"Well, most people don't have the option for an alternative, however, in some cases, there can be. These usually happen when the there is an advocate pleading on behalf of the person. That would be me."

"So you tried to set up a deal for me?"

"Correct. Killing innocents is always frowned upon. However, in your case, those that you have killed have suffered such a fate because they were, essentially, bad guys. It was your duty, as an officer, to remove them from society. Sure, you are a hothead. But, I showed the powers that-be that your actions were for the good of the common man. That you maintained peace in this way. They agreed with me, and because of this, they are offering you an alternative. You won't have to spend the rest of your time-which would be fifty-eight years, in the netherworld."

"I still have fifty-eight years? That means I'd be around

ninety."

"Yes, and that is the problem. You don't want to spend fifty eight years in the netherworld. It's not a very nice place, it's kind of like a purgatory."

"Well, yeah, that definitely doesn't sound so hot. What did you offer them instead?"

"Well, you have to understand that this whole living on earth business is just a part of your whole life. One piece of the puzzle. The real deal happens in the beyond. Right now you're between earth and the beyond."

"Ok, so how do I avoid the netherworld? Can't I just stay here until my time is up? By the way, what do you guys do for fun here anyway?"

"I think you're getting ahead of yourself. This place is designed for brief stays only. There are no "fun" activities. There is peace and contemplation so that you can think with clarity."

"Okay. So how do I make up my time, then?"

"Roger, what I'm about to tell you may not seem like the best solution in the world, but it will shave off a lot of time from your actual stay. You won't even know the time has passed.

"You see, if you stay in the netherworld, you'll have to wait fifty eight years to go to the next level. What I've suggested… is that you return to earth as a cat."

"A cat? This is your grandiose plan to save me from the netherworld? Are you kidding me? What kind of guardian angel are you?, You want me to go back as a friggin cat?"

"Oh dear, I was afraid of this. Calm down Roger, and let me explain. First of all, you don't have to accept it. Second of all, we don't have any other options. If you go back as a cat, you'll probably live all of fifteen years on earth. Fifteen years as opposed to fifty eight. And you won't know you were a man, you will literally live your life as a cat, thinking cat thoughts doing cat things. You won't suffer the agony of being a man trapped inside a cat.

"After your time is up, you return to being a man with no memory of being a cat. Either way, you're not suffering and you're not aware of what's happening. When you come back as a man, you won't know that the time has passed. You'll probably ask me when you would start living as a cat. That's how disconnected one life is from the other. But here's the important thing. It will be fifteen years and then you'll get your wings. You'll go to the next level. That's the real life, not life on earth."

"Hmm. Great." Roger rolled his eyes. "Do you need an answer immediately?"

"No, no, this is the waiting station. You can take your time to think about this. There's a bungalow where you can spend your time here, everything is set up for you. You can rest a little, take in the sights and think of the alternatives. Just don't take too long."

"I have a bungalow?"

"Come on, I'll show you around."

Colin lead Roger outside the white corridor. All around were beautiful gardens, fountains, and ponds. The skies were blue and Roger, who had always lived in New York City, had never seen anything so beautiful.

"Wow, this place is really nice. Are you sure I can't stay here for fifteen years as a man?"

"If I could do it Roger, you know I would. Now here's another thing. You notice that there's no one else around. Everyone here lives on their own frequency. That means you won't see anybody and nobody will see you. It's not a social place, it's a place of change and of direction. All around you, there are others who have similar or dissimilar situations as you."

"You mean, they're all going back as cats??"

"No Roger, that is unique to you. I know it sounds insane, but you'll be living the life of a house cat, a pampered animal. Living quietly in a house. No work. And you won't know you're there."

"Great." Roger said sarcastically. "So, I'm surrounded by people I can't see."

"You're surrounded by spirits in your day to day life on earth, but you're unaware of them. You would find it quite disconcerting if you could see the spirit of someone you had shot in a crime scene. Humans are just not ready for that. You never want to be in a situation where you'll say the phrase, "I see dead people"."

In the midst of this conversation, they had stopped in front of a small structure.

"We have arrived at your bungalow."

Before him was a very nice cottage with honeysuckle vines growing up the side of the house, and a little garden in front and a path that led to the door.

"Hey, this is very nice. Looks like something out of a story book."

"I'm glad you like it Roger. Take some time to think about what you want to do, but don't take too long. Think about the life you've led, the kind of life you'll like to lead, what makes you happy, all the positive things you can think of. You'll have time to pursue them and more after you finish your time. Anyway, I'll let you explore your space, if you need anything just call my name, and I'll return."

"Listen Colin, I'm sure you're trying to help me, but it's going to take me a while to warm up to the idea of spending the rest of my life as a cat."

"It's not the rest of your life Roger, it's just finishing up your former life."

"Whatever, but still, it's not like I'm jumping up and down saying "Hooray, I'm going to be a cat, I'm going to be a cat""

"Well, Roger, you have the time, take all the time that you want to think about this. Just don't take too long."

"Okay, let me look at the place. Can I go anywhere I want to?"

"You're on your own frequency Roger, you can go anywhere you like. Explore the place, you may be surprised at what you find."

Roger began his exploration of the grounds a skeptic, but as he discovered the individual and vacation-like atmosphere of his surroundings, he grew more and more fond of it. It was very much like the place he had always dreamed of for himself, back in the living world.

Roger thought of his father, who had been a cop- how young Roger was when he decided he would be one himself. But that was the other world. The world in which he had plans for himself, but had never slowed his career down enough to do so. He never stopped to smell the daises. He ran. Always ran. He worked hours that would kill most men. His obsession with work ended his first marriage. His first wife had been a good woman, and Roger had been an idiot. And he had continued to be an idiot for a long time after that, never realizing that he'd been such an idiot.

Roger spent about a week in this state. He pondered the life he'd lived before- the errors he had made in that life. He should have known that there was more to life then, before he'd lost it. He even thought about memories that should have stayed locked away in his brain. He'd done terrible things to others, and terrible things had been done to him.

Every day his walks became longer. There was a bench he liked to sit on by a lake. He could look up at the sky and be calmed by it. But always, in the back of his mind was that he had a time-stamp on this paradise, and the expiration date drew nearer day by day. Colin had warned him not to take too long. But Roger didn't know how long 'too long' *was*.

After a week had passed, he'd concluded that going back would not be a boon for him. He was, after all, a marked man. Or would be, once the mob found him alive. And they would. It could take years, but they'd find him.

In his line of work, Roger had tried to be a good man. He'd never taken bribes and always brought the bad guys to justice. And justice, in the 1940's was not a goal reached by accepting bribes.

There's gotta be something more than this, he thought. He remembered the potential of fifty-eight years in the netherworld. That would be purgatory. Literally.

But becoming a cat…

He wouldn't remember anything of it. And life as a cat couldn't be terrible. It would only be for fifteen years- a fraction of the time he'd otherwise spend in the netherworld. He thought of being a fluffy house cat. He'd never have to work. Free meals, attention from someone who would love him. He'd just laze around for the span of his life.

Maybe it wouldn't be terrible.

Roger pictured himself small and soft, curled into the lap of a loving child while sun from a nearby window warmed his fat, well-fed belly.

He summoned Colin.

"Colin, I've made my decision. I'm going to go with your suggestion and live out the remainder of this earth life as a house cat. I'm not going to lie to you, I think this is very strange, but inasmuch as I've no idea what goes on in the netherworld, I got a feeling it's going to be a lot like my old life, or worse. These days that I've been alone I admit, looking back on my old life, it wasn't that hot to begin with. I could have made better choices, done things differently, but I wasn't educated and never had much guidance. I just emulated my father. I didn't know what I was getting myself into."

"Roger, I'm glad you chose the cat life. I understand perfectly that on the surface, it truly doesn't seem like much, but it will go quickly and then you can get your wings. However Roger, I must tell you that for every day that passes here in the waiting room ten years have passed by on earth and now we're seventy years into the future."

"What? You mean to tell me that while I've been here, life has been passing me by? Why didn't you tell me that this was happening, why didn't you explain everything? Is there anything else you've left out,? Is there going to be another shoe that's going to drop?"

"Roger, you needed to detox. Now be completely honest with me and with yourself, have you not had great revelations about yourself and your life in the past week? Have you not seen yourself in a way that you've never seen yourself before? Have you not seen all the things you could have done better, that you shouldn't have done at all? Tell me that didn't happen and I will apologize for forgetting to mention the time difference."

Roger rubbed his chin and sighed.

No, you're right, I've viewed my life with more clarity and seen all of the things that never worked for me, I've seen more here than I had my whole life."

"That's the purpose of the waiting station, you're here to reinvent yourself. The time difference doesn't matter because your time down there is going to be brief. Think about it, only a day and a half will go by here while you're living your new life down there, and then you'll be back here, exactly where you left off. But you'll be going to the next level of your evolution. The cat existence is a minor detour, but your presence will bring joy and happiness to a person's life, a person that needs you, Roger, to be in their life."

"I don't know how I'm going to bring joy to another person. How am I going to adapt to the future?"

"Roger, you're going to be a cat and all you need to know is you're going to be living in a house and somebody is going to take care of you, and you're going to take care of them just by being a cat. I know that doesn't make any sense, but believe me, it will take care of itself. I will step in from time to time to make sure that things are working out for you."

"What could possibly go wrong?"

"Nothing, really, but there might be a few hiccups now and then. Just little tweaks that are needed to make things harmonious. I've found someone who is going to be very much in tune with you, so you'll have the best possible life there. It's not a random event where just anybody is going to take you. A certain somebody is going to take you."

"You already know who this person is."

"Yes, while you've been here detoxing, I've been doing my homework."

"Even though it's seventy years into the future?"

"Roger, trust me, I'm a guardian angel, I have certain abilities that are stronger than those of any mere mortal. No matter how far in the future it is, I've found a great lady to take care of you."

"Is she cute?"

"Roger her physical appearance is not germane to the issue, because you'll be a cat, however to answer your question with the same colloquial expression of your vernacular, yes, she is "cute"."

"Colin, why can't you speak English like everybody else?"

Colin rolled his eyes and shook his head. "That *was* English, Roger."

"Okay, I trust you found somebody good to take care of me as a cat. I'm still confused, I don't know what I'm in for and knowing that I'm dead is not making things any easier."

Roger looked at Colin, an eyebrow raised.

"So how does this cat thing work? Is it going to hurt? do I have to drink something to turn into a cat?"

"No Roger, nothing like that. You are a spirit and you will inhabit the body of a cat. The moment that happens, you will forget that you're Roger Fahey, former NYPD detective and become Roger the cat. By the same token, that cat body will be transformed by your spirit. You may be bigger than most cats. You'll think cat-like things and act like a cat. Every now and then you may do something that is peculiar for a cat, because that will be your spirit coming through. But you won't be aware of it, it will just happen."

"Alright, let's get this over with, and start my life as a cat, 'cause otherwise, I may back out of it."

"That's the spirit!" said Colin.

CHAPTER ONE

I was racked with guilt and grief as I spread the Tarot cards for the twentieth time. Each time, there were slight variations but the message was basically the same: this was the beginning of a positive change that would benefit me.

I'd been doing tarot cards for over fifteen years and I knew the cards weren't lying to me.. I was just punishing myself for the move I was finally about to take. Life had been kind of hard for me, Mandy Cummings, for the past ten years.

My beautiful Fluffy died seven years ago. Fluffy was my angora cat who'd been with me for just about forever. However, all good things have to come to an end, and Fluffy held on as much as possible, but he finally had to throw in the towel. He passed, and his death left a gaping hole in my heart.

I couldn't bring myself to replace Fluffy with another cat. Which is what all this commotion with the Tarot cards had been about.

My friend Jill, who is the most well-meaning person on earth, even if she's sometimes clueless how she may be affecting people, tried to get me a cat. She worked part time at an animal shelter, and after the first year of Fluffy's death, she tried to convince me to get another cat. She just couldn't understand that this wasn't like getting a new washing machine, when the old one broke. Non-cat people never understood.

Even seven years after Fluffy died, Jill urged me to move on. "Fluffy would understand. He'd smile down on you from heaven if you adopted another kitty."

I preferred creatures to humans. But it wasn't always that way.

One morning, five years ago, my husband left for work. A morning like any other. I'd made a pot of coffee and curled up with a book in my hands, and Fluffy in my lap. I sat on the padded bench beneath our bay window. The sun streamed in though the blinds, and warmed my arms, as well as Fluffy's belly. I wasn't expecting a call. I wasn't expecting anything.

But I got the call. The call a person dreads their entire life. I knew even before I picked up the phone. My hands shook, and Fluffy wrapped his tail around my leg in a fashion that I took to be protective.

The voice on the other end was so far away. It was like I was at the top of a deep well, and the man on the phone was so far beneath me. But I heard his words: "Daniel's dying, Mandy. You'd better come quick."

I don't remember how I got to the hospital. The moments between when I heard the news and when I arrived at his room were blurred in my brain. An amalgamation of colors and sounds. Nothing to them, really.

He was dead by the time I arrived. Covered in a white sheet in a hospital bed. So small, shrunken.

He had been on his way to work and had collapsed outside of his office building. Heart attack at forty-eight.

No history of heart disease.

People don't just die like that. At least, in my world they didn't. But Daniel did. The person I loved most in my life died, and I was alone. I determined never to remarry, or date. These wounds ran deep and even Jill knew better than to cross that line. She had thankfully been mum suggesting anything about male companionship. Besides, I had my friends. They weren't going anywhere and no one has disappeared from my life since then.

I flipped another card. I hoped that they wouldn't indicate that a new cat was a good option. Maybe that was just the coward in me talking. I felt guilty that I was betraying my Fluffy whenever I even looked at any other cat that I thought was even cute on social media or on the web. Now, Jill had finally talked me into actually going down to the animal shelter and picking out a new cat. She said there was no pressure, if by chance I didn't like it after a couple of days I could always bring it back, I was not committed to keeping it.

However, I may have to bring it back. I had no idea how I would react when I brought a new cat into the house. A kitten, would be too much work. I needed a young cat that was going to stick around for a while. I also hated the idea of having to bring back some poor animal if it didn't work out. I would be heartbroken if that happened. This was really hard on me.

I gathered the courage to get away from the desk, from the tarot cards and go to the animal shelter. The cards had suggested that today would be a good day. At least, I had that in my favor. I also had in my favor that today that Jill had put up a sign that said the animal shelter was opening late, so I would have the place to myself for a half hour

I looked for my car keys and fought my habit of many years of turning the television set on for Fluffy before I left. I had the silly idea that he would feel like he had a companion that way.

I left the house and electronically unlocked my car. I opened the door and slid in. I looked at myself in the rear view mirror, since I'd forgotten to do so at home, I was so pre-occupied with going to the animal shelter. But as I looked in the rear-view mirror, my brown eyes looked back at me and I could see that my auburn, shoulder length hair was in place and I was wearing a blouse and skirt that wouldn't embarrass me in public.

One of the things that set me apart from most of the people in this town was that I did tarot card readings professionally and also created astrology charts for requesting customers. In my small town and county, I was known as the tarot card lady, since I mostly did these at restaurants and at the mall. From these readings I would also get clients that would hire me to do astrological charts. When Daniel had been alive it was great because this was a way for me to bring in some extra money and do something I really loved. Daniel had been very supportive of me and knew that this was important to me.

Since Daniel had died, things had been difficult for me financially. He'd set up a living revocable trust and had done well managing our finances. Still, it wasn't enough for me to live on. I had to work as a temp to make ends meet. I wanted a full-time position, but the market was saturated with young professionals, and I wasn't exactly one or the other. I'd been a stay-at-home wife who worked with Tarot cards and astrology on the side. I hadn't anticipated that I'd need full-time work.

My literature degree didn't amount to much in today's world. I would get jobs as an admin and as office manager but they were always temporary jobs. Some would last for months, but they never hired me in full-time. Lately though, I'd felt my fortune was about to turn. My current place of employment seemed as though they would offer me a full- time position. I could then have enough money for everything on a regular basis.

It was hard to not distract myself. I had so much on my mind. I turned the car on and headed to the shelter. I couldn't put this off any longer. As I placed my hands on the steering wheel, a call came in on my phone. Jill.

"Hey, I was calling just in case you had changed your mind."

"No Jill, I'm in the car right now and I'm getting ready to head over. I appreciate you letting me in early."

Jill said, "Okay. I just wanted to make sure."

***

After they both hung up, Jill did a little happy dance because she was finally getting Mandy to come to the animal shelter to pick out a new cat. She wasn't going to be pushy or anything, she was just going to let fate guide Mandy to her new cat. Jill was just hoping that Mandy wouldn't chicken out and leave without a cat. That was her biggest fear. There were so many cute cats in the animal shelter at this time, that this is why she wanted Mandy to come early so she could have the pick of the litter. She didn't want her to get distracted or get spooked by too many people. In short, she didn't want Mandy to have any excuses for not a getting a cat.

She felt really bad for Mandy. She had been alone for a quite a while and she knew that Mandy hadn't been happy for a long time. They knew each other since high school and knew Mandy to be a happy go lucky free spirit. But for a number of years now, she felt her friend had gotten tarnished and she wanted her to glow again. It may not be the glow of the past but at least it was the glow of a new beginning in her life. She thought that a new cat could start opening doors in Mandy's life.

***

I drove down the highway on the way to the animal shelter. I felt lighter now as I drove down the highway and closer to the shelter. All the drama of the morning was a sort of catharsis and now that I knew I couldn't back out of my commitment, I was in a zen-like state. I felt that that day could be the start of something nice in my life.

And it wouldn't be just a little reward. It would be a thing that would have permanence.

The right cat could be the answer to a lot of things. I just hoped that the right cat was in there. But you know what, if the right cat isn't in there today, there will be other animal shelters, other cats and other days. I'll be sure to take Jill with me to keep me honest if I had to hunt around. However, right now, I'm in this energy zone where I'm certain that there is a cat out there for me. Why didn't I think of this before?

***

Colin had scoured the country to find the right owner for Roger. He had conducted his search while Roger had been soul-searching in the Waiting Station.

He found a lady who had suffered a lot of loss and sorrow in the last couple of years. She needed a special cat, not just any ordinary cat. Roger would definitely not be an ordinary cat. He knew that this woman would be looking for a cat and he also found out where she would be trying to adopt this cat. So he worked his powers so that there would files in place that gave Roger a history and the necessary papers.

Everything would appear as though this cat had been left at the shelter under circumstances that would seem normal for a pet. It would all seem very natural and nobody would be the wiser that prior to the time he'd been in the animal shelter, Roger didn't even exist in this world as a cat, or as an anything for that matter. But from now on, he would be a cat in this world.

***

Finally, I arrived at the animal shelter. The shelter was a converted warehouse that the city had given to the people who ran the shelter, under the condition that they maintained the building and did all the things that were necessary to keep a building from deteriorating. There had been a lot of volunteers that helped out and in the end, it was their efforts that resulted in a very nice shelter. Jill waited for me outside. When I got out of the car, Jill ran over and gave me a big hug.

"I'm so excited, I'm so happy that you're finally going to have a new kitty in your life." she said.

"Take it easy, Jill. Baby steps. Let me catch my breath and come to terms with the fact that I'm here."

Jill stepped back and apologized,

"I'm sorry, my enthusiasm got the better of me."

I knew Jill very well and when it came to things like this, Jill was everyone's cheerleader. She would egg people on and give a push when they felt apprehensive, not knowing that sometimes people just needed their space. But she always meant well, and people knew that, so no one stayed mad at her for long.

Not having been at the shelter I looked around the place. There was a lot of space and the cages were strategically placed so that the animals were not on top of each other. This had been done as a labor of love. Seeing so many nice animals filled me with warm fuzzy feelings as I walked around the shelter.

One corridor was filled wall-to-wall with many dog breeds. Some were really cute as they hopped around their cages. Although some were puppies, there were also older dogs. I like all animals but for me the perfect animal is always going to be a cat. There's just something about those beautiful furry creatures that have always drawn me to them. And that was the area I wanted to go to, where they kept the cats.

I asked Jill where the cats were.

"I'll bring you to them," Jill said.

She led me down another corridor, which was filled with smaller cages. All of them contained a cat. I reminded myself that I needed to keep an open mind. Except when it came to cats that reminded me of Fluffy. I needed a cat that I connected with, but that did not resemble Fluffy. I resolved to let my gut guide me to the right one.

The cats were mostly sleeping or being quiet, but that gave me time to explore them up close without bothering them. I looked in one cage and there was a sleeping tortoiseshell that looked like it had been overfed. No doubt previously belonging to a zealous owner who couldn't deny her animal treats. In another cage, there was a beautiful Siamese. They were beautiful, but I lacked a connection with them.

***

Colin stood by Roger's cage. The transition had been complete. Roger had no clue about his past life and now he was at the cat shelter. He knew that Mandy would be great for Roger and vice versa. He watched Mandy in the distance. walking closer to Roger's cage. She had her back to Roger and as she was looking at another sleeping cat in the cage across from Roger's. Colin sent a mental command for Roger to meow. Roger performed his first meow.

***

I viewed the sleeping cats. How could I choose just one? At that moment, I wanted them all.

A low, plaintive meow came from my right. I turned to see the source, and before me was a lovely grey tabby.

"Hey baby. Are you calling out to me? Wow, you're a big cat."

At the sound of my voice, the tabby stood and arched his grey back against the cage so that I could pet him. He purred when I touched him, and I thought of how clearly this creature needed love.

"Hey Jill, you know anything about this cat? The big grey tabby?"

Jill ran to me.

"Which one? Which one?" she yelled. She seemed to

catch herself, and by the time I had pointed the cat out to her, she at least appeared to be relaxed.

"You know, he must be new. Huh. Haven't seen this little guy before," Jill said, "I'll check the office for his information."

Jill returned with a blue, laminated card that read 'Roger' in a light, cursive font. Jill turned the card over and read the information printed on the back.

"It says here that he came yesterday. He belonged to an old lady that could longer take care of him, and no other family members who would take him. It also says he's a year old. Wow, he's a big cat for a year old."

I looked at the Roger closely and Roger looked back at me. Our eyes locked for what seemed like a whole minute. I knew in my gut that this cat was special. I could have gone to a whole bunch of other shelters and looked at dozens of cats. But I had just seen ten other cats. and none of them did anything for me. There was something different about Roger. As the words came out of my mouth I couldn't believe that I was saying them.

"You know what Jill, I'm taking Roger home."

Jill said, "Ok, let me go get the papers so that we can make this copasetic."

Jill calmly walked towards the office, but I knew that inside, she was thrilled. I was certain that the moment she closed that office door, she did a happy dance.

I, too, was tempted to dance. I'd gotten a companion. I wouldn't be alone anymore.

CHAPTER TWO

I filled out the paperwork necessary for adoption, still in disbelief that I was a cat owner once again.

Roger, I thought. It would take a while before I would be used to calling him that. I hoped that I would never call him 'Fluffy'. The differences between them were obvious enough. I was sure I wouldn't slip.

I knew I would take Roger everywhere. I used to walk Fluffy around the neighborhood on a leash, and he adored walking the streets with me. Roger would learn to be a constant companion, too. No stay-at-home cat for me. He'd be with me always.

First things first though. I needed to buy supplies for Roger. I didn't have any cat supplies at home, and it hurt too much to keep around Fluffy's old stuff. So I was going to buy Roger all new stuff. I wanted Roger to feel right at home from the very first day.

Jill had always thought it strange that I would walk Fluffy on a leash, and she could see I was going to start doing the same thing with Roger. I put the collar on Roger, and he didn't flinch. I walked him around the animal shelter and he was fine, like he had been doing this all his life. He was a good cat. It was hard to believe he was a year old, but the papers didn't lie. He was also very muscular for a cat, certainly a strange tabby. I took him outside and he liked being in the sun.

I was pleasantly surprised that Roger took to the leash without a fight. He walked about and explored the parking lot. The leash gave him space to observe-and adjust to- his surroundings.

I turned to Jill.

"I was so nervous about getting a cat. You should have seen me this morning. I was a wreck. But, I'm glad I came. Roger is a real treasure, and if it weren't for you prodding me, I wouldn't have done this," I said.

She gave me a hug. "I'm so happy for you, I knew for years you deserved a nice kitty, someone to keep you company and that you could take with you wherever you went."

Jill was always trying to help, even if sometimes she ended up making matters worse. But that day, she'd done well for me. I let Jill go back to work, and Roger and I headed to my car.

He was a healthy cat, and while he was attached to the leash he had a strong pull-almost like that of a dog. I made a note to be vigilant that he wouldn't pull my arm from its socket if he got excited over a bird.

Roger sat in the backseat. He explored the upholstery, sniffed around the corners of the door, and eventually settled down enough to peer through the closed window at the grounds outside.

The drive to the mall was relaxed and easy. It was early enough that traffic was slow.

I'd decided to visit my friend, Wendy, at her store:

Wendy's Pet Cutie Supplies. Wendy had been a fixture in that mall for years. Many folks visited Wendy's for their pet's needs, and also because Wendy was known for having unique merchandise. The big chain stores had nothing on the personal touch Wendy afforded her customers, and being an animal lover herself, she was great at anticipating her customer's needs.

I found a spot close enough to the store and parked my car.

"Roger honey, we're here, we're going to get you nice stuff so that you can feel at home."

I was excited to see Wendy again. It had been years, and I was sure she would be thrilled to see that I'd adopted a cat. At that point, I was still adjusting to that fact myself.

I opened the car door, expecting Roger to be fearful of the world. But he immediately hopped out of the car, his nose stuck up and his little nostrils flared, as if to appreciate the freshness of the outside air.

I grasped the leash, prepared to attach it if Roger attempted to flee. He didn't He didn't wander far, and mostly sniffed at the new space he found himself in. What a wonderful cat he was. I counted myself lucky to have snapped him up.

I made sure the doors were all locked, and as I turned around to enter the store, a disheveled man in filthy clothes approached me. My heartbeat quickened, but I tried to maintain the appearance of stoicism.

"Hey lady, can you spare some change, I really need to get something to eat."

A pan-handler. That's all he was. Still, I didn't quite feel at ease. I dug through my purse, knowing full well I wouldn't find cash. I paid for everything with my phone, or credit cards.

"Sorry" I said, "I really don't have any change on me."

"Ah c'mon you gotta have something, I need to get some change just to get some breakfast, I'm not asking for much just some change."

He had raised his voice and I realized he was crazy. He was bigger than me and I wasn't sure I could run away fast enough. Luckily there were other people around who had heard the man yell, and they watched my interactions with him.

He continued to harass me for money, and once he figured out that he was getting nowhere with that, he changed his tune:

"Hey you know what, you look sexy."

He reached out touched one of my breasts. I gasped and then screamed.

"Don't you dare touch me again, or I'm calling the police."

The other parking lot occupants began to defend me as well. Several of them warned him to leave me alone, while others taunted him by recording the ordeal on their phones. The man took no notice, obviously so engrossed in his own world, he couldn't perceive them.

"Yeah, you look hot, come here."

He reached out to grab me again. All of a sudden Roger jumped onto the guy's arm and started to scratch and bite him. He did it with so much force that he knocked the guy over and continued his attack.. The only sound in that parking lot was the growl of an angered beast. Roger was that beast. I pulled on the leash and said:

"Roger, honey, leave him alone."

The guy was screaming

"Get him off me, I'm allergic to cats!"

He was coughing and sneezing. I tried to pull Roger off as much as I could, but he was still clinging on to the bum's t-shirt. In the distance I could see mall guards coming to help, apparently someone had reported this to them.

More and more people gathered round.

One woman told me, "Don't worry, I got the whole thing on my phone if you're going to press charges."

I could hear police sirens in the distance, apparently someone had called the police as well. Incidents like these didn't happen often in Pleasant Falls, so people got involved.

Some of the witnesses were stunned at how courageous Roger had been. They'd never seen a cat attack a person who harmed their owner. I was still in shock that I'd been assaulted in the mall parking lot. The fact that a cat-my new cat- had leapt out to save me...it was too much to process at the time.

The police arrived, slapped handcuffs on the pan-handler, and took him away. An officer remained on the scene to question me, but I was much too shaken to answer. I told him that I would come by the station and make an official statement once I'd gathered myself.

Roger sat on the ground, calm as could be, licking a paw as if nothing at all had happened.

On my way into the mall, I recognized one of my friends-Jimmy-who was standing by a door, waiting. Jimmy was a local police officer who I knew since high school.

"Mandy, you need to go to the station and make a statement," he said.

"You know Jimmy, I'm still pretty freaked out about this guy touching me out in the parking lot, let me calm down for a while and I'll make a statement at the mall and then go down to the station."

Then he saw the cat and said, "Did you get a new cat? After all these years? Wow !

"Yes, he protected me from that creep."

The pan-handler sat in the back seat of the cop car. Even through the window of the cruiser I could see the scratches Roger had left on his arms. The sound of the pan-handler's sneezes could be heard where I was standing on the parking lot.

"Jimmy, you're going to have to get your car disinfected afterwards, that guy is sneezing up a storm in there."

"Yeah, he's pretty disgusting. We already got a read out on him - he was in jail before. I don't know what he's doing out. Come over the station later, ok?"

"Sure thing Jimmy. I just need to relax for a while and buy some new things for my new cat."

I finally made it into Wendy's place and she could see that I was still shaken up. She also saw the cat.

"Mandy, are you ok? I heard about what happened out there. Wow, you managed to get a new cat after all these years! How wonderful. What's her or his name?"

"His name is Roger."

"What happened out there? I heard you had some kind of altercation."

I told Wendy everything that had happened. I finished my story with Roger's heroics.

Wendy said, "Some cats are very protective of their owners, but I have never heard of a newly adopted cat doing this. He must know people well. He looks like a tabby, but he's so big, there's some other breed in there, maybe a Maine Coon, that might give him these qualities. In any event, it's great that you got a new cat, he's really a cutie."

Wendy, I need everything for a new cat, I'm going to put my faith in you in knowing exactly what to get. I know I haven't been here for a while, but the place looks great and I'm sure you'll get some great things for Roger."

"Oh Mandy, it will be my pleasure. One of my favorite things is getting all the necessary supplies for new pets. It's so important to get just the right things so that they feel at home in their new environment. Follow me."

As she was saying she took me around the store so I could pick out different shades and which styles I liked better. After what had just happened I was truly getting the best for Roger, he deserved it. He just proved his loyalty to me, not 15 minutes out of an animal shelter. Stuff like this just doesn't happen every day.

***

After buying supplies, I stopped at the security station at the mall to make my statement and speak well of the guards at the mall. They had responded right away. Who knows what may have happened if they hadn't come in time? . I minimized Roger's role in the situation, I didn't want him to get too much attention. You just never know with these cop types if all of a sudden they suspect that Roger created the situation in the first place. But no, nobody asked about Roger and I made it out of there right away. Next stop would be the police station.

The station wasn't far from the mall. I parked in the parking lot of the municipal building and went to the station. I was very friendly with everyone there. Pleasant Falls was a small town and I had grown up with many of the cops. When in high school, I had dated the captain, Fred Jones for about a year. . We went our separate ways, but stayed friends.

I met Daniel in college, and around the time that I'd found Daniel, Fred had found himself a woman. They married shortly after they'd met, and divorced shortly after they'd married. Daniel and I heard many sordid tales of how Fred's ex-wife had gone behind his back with other men.

But I wasn't sure that was why Fred divorced her. I think it was because she simply wasn't the woman he had hoped she would be. She disappeared after their divorce, and Fred has been single ever since.

I figured that since I was at the station, I would drop by and say hello to Fred-after I'd made my statement to Jimmy.

There was a reception desk directly inside the police station. I approached the receptionist who merely pointed down a hall and said:

"Jimmy's in his office. He's been waiting for you."

She was right. Jimmy was at his desk, doing paperwork that I assumed was for the caper at the mall that day.

"Hi Jimmy, I came by to make my statement."

He said, "Oh you're here. Just take a chair. I'm still filling out the papers on the derelict of the day."

He gave me some papers regarding the event and I filled them out. When I finished I gave him the papers and he looked them over

"What time do you think this whole incident happened Mandy?"

"I figure about eleven A.M."

"Are you ok, head-wise? I know it's pretty heavy, having some guy attack you like that."

"I was freaked out for a while, but I've calmed down. It's just hard to believe that a man would grab my breasts, uninvited, and then return for seconds. Luckily, my cat intervened"

"So, your new cat is an attack cat, huh?" and he let out a chuckle "He looks like a real Tomcat - strong and sure of himself."

Jimmy understood my attachment to Roger right away because he'd seen me and Fluffy together a lot, so he thought nothing of it. He was also a cat person, himself, so he didn't find my situation peculiar.

"Jimmy, is Fred around? Thought I'd poke my head in to say hi," I asked.

He said "Fred's out investigating a suicide."

"A suicide? In these parts? That's so strange."

"Yeah, don't know much about it, I had to answer the call at the mall. Fred left before me"

"Well I'll catch up with him the next time. How's your cat doing by the way?"

"She's doing okay. She's getting up in the years though. I hope she sticks around for a long time, but you never know. I was thinking of getting her a young playmate so that if she passed away I would still have a cat and there wouldn't be much of an adjustment phase."

I knew Jimmy was practical and although he loved his cat, he didn't have the same relationship with his that I had with Fluffy. Still, I was glad that his cat was still alive and well.

Roger and I left the police station and strolled the area around the municipal building. People kind of looked at us as we walked by, seeing a cat being walked on a leash, but I didn't mind. I was used to it from so many years with Fluffy.

I was overcome by a pang of guilt. But it passed quickly as I reminded myself that Fluffy had been gone for seven years at that point. Roger was a very special cat, and with him, I was gifted a new beginning- just like the tarot cards had said.

It was time I headed home and introduced Roger to his new environment.

I looked forward to playing with Roger for the first time. I had even bought a toy bird for him that could be attached to a string so that Roger could try to catch it. I found laser-pointers to be mean- the cat would chase the thing all over and never really catch anything.

It would be just the two of us. A new beginning.. Things were looking up, the job, a new cat.I'd been getting more calls for my astrology charts and I had one day at week at a restaurant doing tarot cards. Things were going my way for a change.

The place where I was working now was an art gallery. It was a cool place to work at, with nice people. and I had managed to get my artist friend David Towsky a showing there. When I first got the idea for an art show for David, I talked to the owner, Bernard Jakovsky, at length and told him about David and how he had been a painter for years, could he look at his paintings, and they had hit it off. Bernard really liked David's art and saw that his paintings had a lot commercial potential. Bernard agreed that this was definitely show material, and that show was going to happen next week. I felt that the world was going to get to see more of David's art and hopefully he would sell some works and it would open new doors for him. I was really excited about that.

Finally home, I set up Roger's things and let him explore the house so that he could get acquainted on his own terms.

I was putting stuff away and my phone rang. I saw that it was Jill calling.

"I have some good news and some bad news."

I heard this and I didn't like it, but I wasn't going to let my good mood be ruined so, I'd just focus on the good news.

"Ok tell me the good news.

"Do a search on YouTube for *cat protects owner at mall*."

I did the search and right away a video came up of Roger protecting me at the mall. It already had a couple hundred views.

I laughed, "That's amazing, who put it up?"

"Another social media nut like me. I don't know them."

I yelled out, "Roger, come look. You're a hero. People are talking about you."

Then Jill said, "Listen I don't know how to say this, but there's some bad news too."

"Please don't let it be anything about Roger."

She said no, "It's not about Roger, there are no problems with him. It's about David Towsky. David committed suicide."

CHAPTER THREE

The news of David's death hit me like a slap.

David had been a great friend of mine. He was a very talented painter, and we'd known each other for years. I'd never known him to be depressed. Hell, I'd hardly seen him frown.

"What do you mean that David has committed suicide? He had everything going for him. He was getting a showing at a gallery, doing work on a regular basis. Last time I saw him, he was the happiest he'd been in a long time. And now you tell me that he's committed suicide. Something just doesn't add up here."

"I find it completely surreal. I still don't believe that it's true."

"There's no reason why he would commit suicide. Who says he committed suicide and how did he do it?

"The police are saying he died of an opioid pain killer overdose."

"Wait a second, that is just not true. First of all, I know that David is allergic to those types of drugs and he wouldn't take that in a million years, not for medical reasons, not for recreational reasons. Second of all, David had no reason to kill himself, his life was going just great. I'm going to have to visit Fred and find out how he came to this conclusion because I don't believe for five minutes David committed suicide. This was either an accident or somebody killed him and there's nothing in between.

"Mandy, how could you be so sure? After all, David was an artist and artists have been known to be mentally ill, and to abuse drugs. Maybe there was some deep dark secret that he didn't want anybody to know about and having all this success just made it worse and he couldn't take it."

"Oh Jill, David wasn't one of these deep, dark and heavy souls. If it wasn't for his art, he'd be a ditz. He always had his head in the clouds thinking about art. In that respect I agree with you, he was an artist and he was slightly nutty, but not the type that brooded about life and was constantly seeing the glass half empty. So no, I may not have known everything about David, but I knew this much, David wouldn't so much as hurt a fly, let alone kill himself."

"This just sounds to me that the police have no idea why he's dead and this seems like a good theory. Which is crazy because that is going to break his mother's heart. I forgot, Margot must be beside herself with grief. David had moved back here to be close to her in her old age, and they had formed a great bond over the last couple of years. News that her son committed suicide would make her question everything. And she would somehow blame herself. Anyway, I have to make a couple of phone calls, this just doesn't make sense. I'll talk to you later Jill, and I'll tell you all about the stuff I got Roger."

Hands shaking, I hung up with Jill. I sat for a moment, unable to think, before I decided to call David's mother. After many rings, I was prompted to leave a message. I don't know how I managed to make a sound, but I did.

"Hi Margot , It's Mandy. I am devastated by the news. I will call or visit tomorrow."

I felt terrible about bothering Margot, but I was certain she could use a friend. At that time, I needed a friend just as badly. I stared at my phone for a long time, still reeling at the fact that David was dead.

I thought back to my college days when I first met David. He was good looking, artistic and a gentle soul. I was dating Daniel and I thought that David would make a perfect boyfriend for Jill. He was a little flighty and so was she. There was only one problem that I discovered shortly after I mentioned Jill to him. He was gay, so hooking him up with Jill wasn't going to fly. But we developed a friendship and I would go to see his art shows, however small they were. He was a good artist and I have always been a supporter of the arts, so it worked out. He lived in New York City for a while, but he moved back here to be close to his mother.

This being labeled a suicide just didn't make sense. There had to be more to his untimely death. Who would want to kill David? It's not like he had enemies. He was mellow, level headed, lived with his boyfriend, Harold, with whom he had broken up with recently, but it was an amicable parting.

That's what David said. Maybe it wasn't as amicable as I thought. Maybe Harold was crazy with jealousy and grief. Breakups can really bring out the freak in people and who knows, maybe Harold went off the deep end?

I needed to calm down. Allowing my imagination to run wild would be of help to no one- least of all myself.

Fred. I needed to call Fred. It didn't matter how busy he was with paperwork. He would listen to me.

After a couple rings, Fred picked up.

"Mandy, I'm picking up this call because I know that David was close to you, but I'm very busy with paperwork and all the legal ends."

"Okay Fred. I just have to know - why is it being labeled a suicide?"

"There was no sign of conflict or violence. We found a glass of water by his bed with the substance in it."

"Was this an opioid painkiller?"

"Yes, I guess the press got a hold of that."

"Okay Fred, listen to me. David was allergic to opioid pain killers, he would never take this in a hundred years. His life was turning around. Everything was going great for him. Why would he kill himself? Can't you re-access what's going on? I don't know why anybody would kill David, but I'm telling you this is not a suicide."

"Mandy, sometimes the people that we think we know are people we don't really know completely, especially if they have a dark side. Sometimes that dark self comes out and does ugly things. I see it every-day, seemingly nice people do horrible things. It's possible David was one of them and you just didn't know, I'm sorry Mandy. I have to go, please don't jump to any conclusions, I really think that this is suicide, nothing mysterious here."

After we'd hung up, I sat on my bay window bench and thought over what Fred had said. It was true that many people had a dark side. Maybe David did, too.

There were likely all kinds of professionals involved-It wasn't just Fred investigating David's death- there were specialists, coroners, people who studied the crime scene and gathered evidence.

So far, nothing pointed to foul play. I thought of consulting my tarot cards. David was supposed to have done an art show that coming weekend that I'd also forgotten to do a reading of. I was so preoccupied with

Roger, I'd forgotten.

Could there be a connection between the show and his death? Could a jealous artist have murdered David? It would have to be somebody that knew him well or a rival artist.

Even though I was an emotional wreck, I had to try to do a reading to see what the cards would say. I know 90% of the world would think I'm nuts for looking at Tarot cards at a moment like this, but if I can keep calm, I might get an idea of why my gut keeps saying that it's not a suicide.

All this while, Roger had been sleeping in the chair opposite me. He had adjusted very well to the house. At least something was going right.

***

'I walked about the room and lit my candles. After drawing the curtains closed, I slid a large pillow from beneath the tarot table and sat down. I spread the cards before me in a five-card horseshoe spread, reluctant to look. I reached across the table to turn them overand see what message they held about David. The cards showed that there was something or someone hidden in the background. There was danger, but the danger had already passed, David was dead. But the question is, was this hidden thing something in David's psyche or something in the real world? The cards kept saying something close to David, but I still couldn't figure out if it was his psyche or someone. Or even some thing.

The phone startled me from my meditative state. Which was just as well. I was too emotionally raw to properly conduct a reading. I'd approach it again when I had a clear mind with which to do so.

I grabbed my phone from the kitchen counter. It was Jill.

"Hi, I just called to see how you were doing. I knew

that David's death would be weighing heavy on your mind."

"Well, I spoke with Fred, and he told me that everything pointed to suicide and I begged to differ, but it didn't make any difference. In spite of what Fred said, I still have this gut feeling that something was not right."

"Listen, maybe we should just go out and get a coffee or something to take your mind off this, otherwise you're going to drive yourself nuts."

"That sounds like a good idea. Meet me at Joanie's coffee shop in ten minutes."

***

Joanie's Coffee and Cupcake Shop was one of the more popular places in town. Joanie had decorated it in a retro style, hinting at the early sixties, but with modern touches. It had bright colors, with old fashioned booths topped with Formica, and a black and white tiled floor. You always felt as though you'd stepped back in time when visiting Joanie's.

A person could sit there, order a coffee and pastry and read or use the wi-fi and Joanie wouldn't shoo you out. Joanie was someone else I went to high school with. This had always been her dream to open up her own bakery – coffee shop. I was one of her best customers.

Roger was up and around, rubbing himself against my legs. He was getting used to living here very quickly. I was very glad. I put the collar on him and we went to the car.

I breathed a bit easier once we were inside the coffee show. It felt safe to be around- and talk to- other people. Jill's presence calmed me the most, as it always had.

She knew I needed to get out and about and here we

were talking about Roger. Roger was very calm, He sat on the floor next to our table. No one at the coffee shop was uncomfortable with Roger being inside. I'd often come here with Fluffy when he was alive. But, I'd been cat-less for years, so Roger did come as a surprise to them. Joanie's eyes widened when she spotted him.

"Oh Mandy, you got a new cat, it's so beautiful. Is it a he or a she?"

"It's a he."

"Well that's a very beautiful tabby. He's big too. Good thing you didn't go for a kitten, they're just too much trouble."

Joanie bent down and pet Roger and he basked in the affection. Roger was an animal that needed love. He would allow people to get close to him. But he apparently knew when there was danger too. I guess that's instinctual.

Joanie said, "Sorry to hear about David, I know you two were close friends. It's terrible when these things happen, people killing themselves for no good reason. And he seemed like such a nice quiet man. Who knows why people do the things they do?"

I didn't want to tell Joanie that I'd consulted the tarot cards, or that David was allergic to pain killers. I didn't want to seem even more insane.

The bell above the coffee shop door rang, announcing a customer. I wished I hadn't turned to see those freshly-polished black dress shoes as they scuffed Joanie's tiled floor. But I had. My eyes moved from his shoes to his dark jeans, and from there to his button-down shirt. When his puffy, red eyes caught mine, my throat closed.

Harold. David's ex-boyfriend.

Harold's face fell when he saw me. He strolled across the store to where we sat.

"Oh Mandy, I'm just so heartbroken about David. I

just don't know how this could have happened. We broke up a couple of months ago, and it was my fault, I had been cheating. I went back after a month to see if we could resolve our issues and maybe get back together.

"He told me he'd found someone else, but wouldn't tell me who. I never saw him publicly with anyone else. Neither did any of our mutual friends. I don't know if he was just playing with my head, or trying to get back at me. But David was never that calculating. I keep blaming myself, thinking if we'd been together still, would this have happened? Was there something I could have done to stop this? I just have no idea. He was never the type to take his life, but it just goes to show, sometimes we just don't know the people we love the most."

Harold sat at the end of our table. He hunched over, put his head in his hands and sobbed. Tears rolled down his arm and dampened his shirt sleeves. I felt terrible for him. I felt terrible for all of us.

In an attempt to lighten the mood, we tried to remember the good times that we'd had with David. I recounted some of my experiences while at college and spoke of his early days as an artist and how his professors lauded his ability to paint. Everyone at that table had watched David morph into the accomplished artist he had been. We'd all watched him struggle for years before he found the recognition he'd deserved.

We shared different funny stories that happened to all of us while hanging out with David, he had a great sense of humor. By remembering the good times, we felt less sad about what had happened.

We decided that feeling bad about David dying was not going to help any of us, we remembered the David we loved and we grew up with and that we would keep his memory alive as long as we lived.

That seemed to be a good way to deal with the

situation, and I did most of this for the sake of Harold, who was a bit of a basket case right now, but I could see that Jill had been affected too. She was a good friend of David's as well.

During all this, Roger would switch between the floor and jumping on my lap. He then would put his head on the table, so all you saw was this head sitting on the table. That made us laugh, and in the course of this Harold became aware that I had a new cat and was introduced to him.

It was a relief to be amongst old friends, and to know that we had all turned out just fine. Most of us had found work doing the things we loved, even if we weren't rich. I'd long ago learned that wealth was nothing if the person who held it was miserable.

Jill loved her animals, Joanie loved her shop, and I loved my cards.

It seemed that the good things in life brought happiness, while the bad things-the evil things-were what brought wealth.

The poor and passionate were the ones that brought music, art, and beauty into the world. And maybe that was more important than bringing money into it. Still, life would be much better if the artists of the world were compensated more fairly.

The peaceful thoughts didn't last long, as Harold brought us back to reality. He had a hand curled beneath his chin-his elbow propped up on the table.

"I wish I knew who David had been seeing. I wish I had the peace of mind that before he passed, he was with someone who had loved him. Hopefully someone who had loved him better than I did,' Harold said.

The table went silent. Jill and Joanie put their heads down. I wanted to comfort Harold, but I didn't know what to say. It wasn't like I'd known the guy, either. I couldn't tell Harold that yes, David *was* happy and well-loved before he'd died.

I couldn't tell Harold anything.

CHAPTER FOUR

The next following day was filled with new responsibilities and new ways of looking at my world. Roger was early to rise, and that meant I was too. His mews were higher pitched and shorter than usual. He had perched at the foot of my bed, and his gentle voice woke me. I didn't feel guilty that day. I felt that if Fluffy could see Roger and me right now, he would be happy for us. Fluffy wasn't the one who decided I should be alone- that was me punishing myself. What for, I wasn't certain. But I knew that morning that I was done.

"Is Roger Hungry?" I asked. To my amusement, he mewed back, as if to answer and leapt off the bed.

I fed Roger the generic cat food I'd found at the store, which would have to do until I'd determined what his favorite flavors were. I set down a fresh water dish for him, then headed to work.

The gallery would still show David's art. I was sure the gallery had contingency plans in place for instances such as these. David probably wouldn't have been the first artist to die of an overdose before a show.

***

I got some pastries and coffee from Joanie's place and headed to work like any other morning. As usual, I was the first one there and usually opened up the place, since I had the keys. Most would stroll in late, so somebody had to keep the place open from early, early being 9 AM. Others liked to stroll in at eleven AM, and the owner never got in until 12 noon. He was one of those well to do people that probably had the gallery as a hobby and not because it was such a marvelous investment. Still, it looked like I might be hired here permanently, so I tried to be positive and do as much good in here as I could.

The graphic designer, Katie Wiggins, usually was there early too. Katie was young, quiet, and a little unusual with multi-colored hair, and ripped up jeans, but this was probably her way of being cool. From time to time the owner would instruct her to dress more professionally, but because she mostly worked in the back of the gallery, away from patrons- he didn't press the issue often. I had become friends with Katie. Katie liked that I was an astrologer and read tarot cards. I had done a couple of readings for her and she thought it had helped her out when making a couple of decisions. So we were on good terms.

I sifted through the mail to make sure there weren't any checks in the pile. Most of our clients purchased online and paid with credit cards. Occasionally we'd receive a call from an elderly person-lonely and wanting to speak with someone. We'd guide them through the buying process, inquire about print sizes or frames, and provide our address so they could send us an old-fashioned check.

The Gallery would try to do one show a month, but sometimes it would take as long as two months to do an art show. Seeing that David's stuff was already in the gallery, they would probably have a post memoriam show and leave the pictures up while they set up for their next show. At least that's how I imagined it would be, but I guess I would find out later.

As usual, Bernard arrived to work at noon, somewhat agitated, but that was his typical attitude. He struggled to move about the gallery- a limp from a previous car accident had given him the gait of a man twice his age, sometimes even having to resort to using a cane. He requested an impromptu meeting..

"Good morning everybody, I have an announcement to make." Bernard ambled slowly to the front of the gallery while Katie and I shot one another questioning glances. "We're going to have to cancel David's show."

"What? Why?" the staff murmured.

Bernard answered. "Bad for business. What are we supposed to do? We don't have an artist to discuss the art with the patrons. It would be a memorial service. No. We need to try to get someone-a living person- in here as quickly as possible. It's an unfortunate situation, but the show must go on. So we'll take the paintings down, and set up for some new show in the future."

I could not believe what I was hearing. Cancel David's show? Why? The pictures could hang till they found someone else, which could take weeks. Meanwhile, why the hurry about taking down the pictures? I gotta head this off at the pass.

Somehow, someway I need to get Bernard to see that it would be better for the gallery to have a showing and a memorial, and we could advertise the whole thing on social media. I was going to have to schedule some time with him immediately before any of the pictures were removed. I tried to speak to him.

"Hi Bernard, could I speak with you for fifteen a minute?"

"Not now Mandy, I have a couple of appointments to

attend to. I know you were close to David, you introduced us as a matter of fact, but there's just no business in doing a showing for a dead artist."

I had to bite my tongue. I figured, he's looking at this situation as a business, not from the point of view a person whose dear friend had departed under horrible circumstances. I said, "Bernard give me 20 minutes, I have some ideas that I would like you to consider and they could be beneficial to the business."

I figured include that it would be "beneficial to the business" otherwise this was never going to fly.

He said "Fine. Twenty minutes. I'll be in my office. Come by around two o' clock."

I was relieved that David's paintings would remain displayed-at least for another two hours. I wasn't sure how to persuade Bernard-I didn't have ideas. I just said so because I knew he'd meet with me.

Bernard retreated to his office and shut the door.

"Guys, do me a favor," I said to my coworkers, "leave the paintings up until I speak with Bernard. Please?"

They readily agreed. I was grateful that they were sympathetic. They wished me luck with Bernard.

The staff knew that Bernard was strange, but he wasn't a bad guy. Maybe business was bad and this just didn't sit well with him. Maybe it was just the strangeness of the whole situation. But whatever it was I had to get him out of the mindset that he had to take down David's pictures.

I sat down to formulate a plan. I would get Jill's help-since she was the queen of social media and websites. We would have the show in memoriam. I would create a Facebook page for the gallery and David, showing how the gallery felt motivated to keep the spirit of David's art alive.

David was well-loved by his community. Many people would pay to see his work-even if David wasn't there. It would be good publicity for the gallery.

I devised a plan with Jill to create stories about David on the Facebook page we were creating. We both agreed to advertise the showing on our social media platforms. I planned to tell Bernard these things during our meeting. He would be pleased that I expected no compensation. Bernard loved free advertising. He was cheap like that, even though he had all this money. A very strange character.

But he was the owner, and he was the one that made the final decisions. I had to show him with my project, that people in the future would see him and the gallery as a benefactor of the arts, and as a result, he might get more clients and more people buying from him in the future. He really didn't advertise enough, but he also didn't know how to advertise.

I really thought that between Jill and myself, we could put this exhibit on the map. We'd showcase the art ourselves, have a short memorial, and a few of us would give speeches. Bernard would be happy to give his speech, he loved being the big shot at such an event. We would film the show and the memorial to place on the gallery's site.

I felt great about our ideas. How could Bernard decline such an appeal to his humanity? I was always providing people with different options and paths with my cards. I often showed people that the world was colorful-not black and white. This was my gift, and it was time to use it.

I got my chance to meet with Bernard. He spoke first.

"I don't' know Mandy, this whole dead artist thing has cast a pallor on the gallery. Business isn't doing well to begin with. I didn't need this. Now what am I going to do?"

"Listen Bernard, you're looking at this the wrong way. Nowadays you can turn this experience into something that would bring you more business and, at the same time, show the gallery in a new light."

"Bernard said, "Ok, I'm listening, what do you have?"

"Whenever there's a noble cause, people flock to social media to advertise it. You can create tributes, or ask for the support of the community to turn such a negative thing into something positive. We can create pubic interest in David's show this way."

"Let me stop you right there Mandy, how much is this going to cost me?

"It's not going to cost you anything. I would take charge of the campaign and with the help of my friend, and put together a Facebook page for the gallery and a memorial in honor of David free of charge. My friend is great with social media and she could drive the right kind of traffic to this webpage This would put the gallery in a very good light because even though there was s terrible tragedy, the gallery did the right thing and had the showcase.

During the showcase I give a short speech about David's life, you give a short speech about how David's pictures are an asset to the gallery. We'll film it and put it on the webpage. It will be great publicity for you, for the gallery, and it would show you as a great benefactor of the arts. You will definitely get a surge in business."

Bernard was listening and nodding. Finally he spoke.

"I'll tell you the truth Mandy, I'm still not sold on this 100%. But show me the webpage you and your friend create. I'll see how things look and we'll take it from there. "

"I'll have something solid for you to look at

tomorrow. Please, just keep the schedule for David's showing. Don't retract invitations. And it may not be profitable right off the bat, but it will be in the long term."

Finally Bernard said,

"Okay, we'll talk tomorrow after I see the page.

"Thank you, Bernard. You'll be pleased with the outcome," I said as I closed his office door.

I was excited that even though I didn't get a resounding yes, I didn't get a no either, and I was sure I could get Katie to help me out as well.

I called Jill and told her my plan. She was excited, she knew exactly what to do regarding the Facebook page. Katie was kind enough to lend me a hand, also. She loved my idea, and was thrilled that we could still honor David's memory. We determined that I would be the one responsible for writing the speeches for the event.

Of course, the pessimist in me started thinking as I was walking away. What if this guy didn't like it. What if he changed his mind? He was weird a lot of the time and there was no telling what he might do. Well, I said to myself, if he decides not to have the memorial showing, hopefully there will be pictures of the paintings and we'll post those on Facebook fan page and promote it. That way, not matter what happens, at least David's work will not be forgotten and I'll feel like I did something to honor his memory. I also felt better that I had the help from Jill and Katie. Having help will also bring new ideas to the project, in case things didn't work out the way I had hoped they would.

The rest of the day I was spent filling out orders for previous prints of previous shows and keeping track of who was buying what. It was all pretty mundane, but it was a job and I was still hoping that they would hire me full time.

I could still do my readings on the side for extra money, but at least I would have a steady income. Here again, I didn't' want to get my hopes up, but I had been here three months and so far they liked me a lot and I liked the place and the people. They're all in the arts and they're all sort of quirky and I always gravitated to artsy types all my life, so I felt very much at home. Time would tell but so far it it seemed a strong possibility I would get hired..

***

Finally it came time to go home. I was looking forward to designing the page with Jill. I was also looking forward to hanging out with Roger. Not having had a cat for so long, I had to keep reminding myself that I finally had a cat, so every now and then I would think, maybe I'll do this after work or that after work and then I would say, no I have to go home and feed Roger, I have to go home and take Roger for a walk. Roger was becoming a part of my life slowly but surely. I still missed Fluffy but Roger had been a good choice. We were going to be friends for a long time.

I had the urge to turn my steering wheel in the direction of the police station-to speak with Fred about David again. The need hit me in a sudden, urgent way that I couldn't shake.

But what good would it do? No. I needed to get home to Roger.

Still that nagging feeling inside of me kept telling me that something was off here, that David's death was not a suicide. Maybe when I was calmer I would either do a chart or do another reading of the Tarot cards and see if they hinted at something. Sometimes the things you would least expect came out of these readings. They didn't tell the future exactly, but they made you think about what could be or what could have been. And sometimes you got what had been and that's really what I was after. The truth was out there, but where?

Eleanor Kittering

CHAPTER FIVE

Later that night, after I'd settled in and fed Roger his dinner, I tried calling Margot, David's mother, again. The phone rang about five times before she picked up.

"Hi Mandy.," Margot said. Her voice was strained. She sounded much older than the last time we had spoken

"Hi Margot, I was just calling to see how you were, if you needed any help, and if there was anything I could do?"

"Well Mandy, yesterday was the worse day of my life. I still feel a bit numb. I've heard from so many of David's friends. Their words and support mean so much to me. A lot of people loved David. I don't know why he didn't love himself."

"Oh, Margot. David loved himself. It's possible that this whole thing could have been an accident. When I last saw David, he was thrilled that his art was being recognized. He was happy, Margot. The police had to label it a suicide based on their discoveries. David did not die of misery," I said. I didn't lie for Margot's benefit. David *had* been happy.

There was a sniffle and a pause at the other end of the line. Just that sniffle from a grieving mother brought a mist to my eyes.

"Thank you, Mandy. You were one of David's best friends and I hear in your voice that you loved him. It makes me feel better to think that my son didn't throw his life away for nothing."

"I'm sure we'll find out that it was exactly that," I said. A chill crawled up my spine, but I shook it off. "Have the police left his apartment?"

"Oh yes, they told me I could go in there again if I like. To tell you the truth I have a difficult time with that thought. Even though I have to clean up and pack his things, the thought of doing that for my son is devastating. A parent is not supposed to outlive their children. Why was my son's life cut short?" Margot's voice became distant as a sob tore through the line. She had likely tried to move her phone from her lips to avoid startling me. Even in grief, Margot considered others.

"I don't know Margot. But please, don't even think for a moment that you're going to do this by yourself. When you are ready to work on the apartment I will help with the whole project. If we need more people, I'll get more people. You're not alone in this world Margot. You have me and you have other's that were David's friends. I lost my husband five years ago. He was only forty-eight. Nobody saw that coming. I completely understand sudden death and being left so empty. So whenever the time comes Margot, when you're ready, I'll be there with you."

"Thank you so much Mandy, that makes me feel so much better that I won't be alone doing this. I truly appreciate it. I'm sorry to say, I'm going to have to be going as some of the family have come over and they're helping me plan the funeral. As soon as we know where the showing is going to be, and when, I'll give you call."

"Oh yes please Margot, do let me know and I'll spread the word, to mutual friends and to other of David's friends. I feel much better having had the chance to talk to you."

"Me too Mandy, me too, thank you so much."

Roger rubbed his face against my leg. He had likely sat at my feet while I was talking with Margot. I reached down to scratch Roger's ears, and he rewarded me with a hearty purr. It was wonderful to not feel so alone. And he was such a brave cat.

If David had felt less alone, perhaps his death wouldn't have happened. How far was I from such a fate? If it could happen so suddenly to David, why not me? Why not any of my other friends?

Still there was that nagging feeling inside of me. Had David gotten mixed up with the wrong crowd? What if there was some sinister element to his death that had been overlooked? Could it have been that another artist had been jealous of him? Could someone have given David that pill, claimed it was an aspirin, and then watched as it killed him?

Someone at the funeral might know something. But what? What did I want to know? If a jealous artist killed David? That didn't happen. That was insane. That was something drug dealers in turf wars did – not people with creative tendencies.

I got up from the couch and washed my face. I didn't need more stress at that moment. It was fine. I was grieving. I was just angry that I didn't know David had been sad, that he hadn't told me he was struggling.

I would keep an open mind, an open heart. I would speak with others at the funeral-especially those I didn't recognize. I had to put my negative feelings to rest. I just needed closure.

This was crazy though, trying to think of who might

have killed David. And then I had to think how I was going to approach these people. It's not like I would say, "Hi you look weird or strange and I think you might have killed David, can I talk to you??" That wasn't going to go over very well. No, there had to be a different way to approach people. See if anybody knew anything secret about David. His boyfriend might give a clue as to who David hung out with and if there were any rival artists worth talking to.

I thought about Mike the drug dealer. Maybe he could tell me who bought opioid painkillers from him recently, although I doubted that. But I could show him David's picture and just answer if this guy bought stuff from him. Explain the situation. He knew me from back I high school and he liked me, although when talking about clients, drug dealers were notoriously tight lipped. You're only as good as your discretion. At least I would know if David bought something from him or not. Of course, he could have bought it off someone else. But it didn't hurt to ask. The worst that could happen is that Mike doesn't want to cooperate and that's that.

Then there's also the possibility whether anybody had anything to gain by David's death. I had to explore his will or living revocable trust and see if there was someone that could have benefitted from his death. Maybe there was an insurance policy that nobody knew about. I just felt there had to be something.

At least I'd gotten an idea of how to talk to people I didn't know who might have been up to no good in David's life. I would pretend that I was writing a piece on David as part of a memorial. It wouldn't be a lie, that's exactly what I was doing. But that would give me the chance to talk to all these people who may have known things about David that I didn't know about and things that maybe he had entrusted one of them with.

You know what they say, rattle enough bushes and

eventually, something leaps out. I just hope that whatever leaps out doesn't come after me too. That was the something that was freaking me out. If indeed this turned out to be a murder, this was dangerous, I could get hurt or worse. Well, if I dug up anything that the cops could follow up on, I would take it to Fred.

Or if I came across a conversation that supplied some kind of lead, I would take Jill with me. Two chickens are better than one, it's not like Jill was any heroine. But at least I wouldn't be alone. And Jill was very creative with slightly devious stuff. And of course, bring Roger, although I would never forgive myself if something happened to him. All this thinking was making me crazy. Now I really felt like I was in some noir novel and the killer was onto my snooping and figuring out how the murder happened.

Suddenly there was a knock on the door and I leapt about a foot in the air. Roger came out of his semi sleepy state to see what made that noise. I went to the door and of course, it was Jill. I had asked her to come over and help me with this fan page on Facebook for David.

Jill as usual, had one hand on her cell phone while having a conversation with others around her. She was constantly on her phone and she spent more time looking at her phone screen than actually looking around her. She had an outline of her plan for the Facebook page ready to go.

"Maybe it would be better if we did it on the computer," I said.

"Yeah, we'll have more room," Jill agreed.

We created a fan page for David. We named it Memorial Service for David Towsky at *Jacovich Galleries*. Katie would be over later with art work that she had created for the page, as well as pictures of some of David's paintings. While Jill edited the Facebook page, I was on my laptop creating the text that was going to go on the page for the show.

After a half hour, Katie showed up and brought donuts and coffee for us. She brought her laptop so that she could work with us.

I enjoyed the atmosphere, and being with friends helped ease my troubled mind. Jill and Katie seemed to get along well.

"How long have you been at the gallery, Katie?" Jill asked.

"Well, it's been six months. It's not a bad place to work, I'm not crazy about Bernard, otherwise, it's ok there," Katie replied.

"What's bad about Bernard?" Jill asked.

"I don't know, something about him rubs me the wrong way. Plus one day I caught him looking up Jessica's skirt."

I laughed "Well, anybody can look up Jessica's skirts Katie. I've never seen her with anything but a micro-mini. Because she's short and she's skinny, she still thinks she's 18. But, whenever she stands up on a stool to make copies, the slightest movement forward and you get a spectacular view of her panties"

Jill and Katie both laughed at this. Then Jill said

"Oh wait, I think I've seen her at the mall. She's always shopping at Strawberry's. And in winter, she's wearing those rabbit fur little jackets and walking around with exposed legs in freezing weather."

"Yes, that's her. She's a little past Strawberry now. She's pushing forty and dressing eighteen. She really does it for the attention, I think she's single. But some women don't learn that dressing like that is going to get you the wrong kind of attention. She needs to discover shopping at the big girls' store. By the way, Jill, I emailed you the text for a couple of posts. Let me know if it's too much."

Jill check her laptop "Yes, I just saw that email".

Katie said "I just go to work the way I feel best. And because I just wear a t-shirt and jeans, at first Bernard thought I should dress more corporate. I said Corporate? This is an art gallery and I'm stuck way in the back where nobody can see me. He let it go, I guess he saw that I was not the receptionist. Not that we have one. By the way Jill, I made that art work to the size you mentioned for the Facebook page, let me know if it fits. I'm also sending you the collage of photos of David's paintings"

Katie was recently out of school and I could see why someone criticizing her way of dress might turn her off. Bernard was an older man, an orthodox Jew, he looked older than his years, so he likely had a more conservative view of the world, thinking that women have to come to work wearing crinoline dresses or business suits. I dressed pretty "business-y" with just a skirt and blouse and I blended in pretty well. Roger was sitting next to me on the floor sometimes, then he would go and see what Katie was doing jumping on the table, then over to Jill, and back to me. He seemingly gravitated to where the action was all the time.

Roger drifted from person to person. He seemed to gravitate toward wherever the action was. The girls adored him, and I loved him more by the minute. Even when he decided to step on my laptop and edit my document, it was difficult to be angry with a creature who was simply seeking affection.

***

The final draft of our work looked great. We had accomplished much more than we thought we would in only an hour.

We exchanged high-fives at a job well done. We could only speculate as to how Bernard would react, but we all hoped he would like our work as much as we did.

Jill had more work planned for herself when she got home. She wanted to place ads for the page to give it visibility. So even if Bernard declined our ideas, at least David would have a page that honored him and his talent.

After my friends had left, my mind returned to David. How to track down people who knew him. I thought and thought of ways to meet as many people as I could who had known David. Harold could help. He would know more about the people David had hung around with towards the end of his life.

So far Harold was basically off the list. I had to come up with an angle on how to talk to a diverse number of people that knew David. I thought that maybe Harold could help. I would tell him that I was getting some backstory for David's memorial,. They didn't have to know that this might not happen. Harold would probably know who were the people in David's life that were more likely to have dealt with him on a regular basis.

But wait, I just realized something. David had also painted portraits. Perhaps there was an old customer with a grudge that did David in. Somebody he knew well enough to have him visit at his house. Maybe one of his clients had become his lover. This was a possibility. I had to see if there was a list of clients from the past. I would ask Margot under the guise that I wanted to interview people for David's memorial page.

I picked up my phone before I realized that it was well past midnight. I would call the next morning to see if she'd be able to provide me with a list of David's clients. Then, I'd talk to Harold to find out more about who David had been spending time with.

Harold was a big busybody so he knew all the dirt on a lot of the people. If he said I should stay away from anybody, those are the ones I would interview. They may have had cause to harm David. Maybe it was some kind of revenge thing that went too far. Still I had no motive. It's not like David had money. David was overall a nice person. But maybe David had a dark side.

I guess, at some point, I would learn what happened. But what if I discovered nothing and it turns out that David really did kill himself. That was a reality that I really didn't want to confront. It would mean another person in my life dead. Why did people keep dying on me? First my mother. Then my cat. Then my husband. And now, my friend. Two of the others were understandable, both my mother and my cat died of old age.

My mother had me later in life, when she was in her late forties. It's possible I wasn't supposed to even be born, but once I was, maybe it gave my mother something to do. Who knows what really happened and why my mother had me so late in life. It's not like I had siblings or anything. Whatever it was, I was an only daughter. As a result, my mother died of old age when most other women still had elationships with their mothers.

My cat, beautiful Fluffy also died of old age. I looked over at Roger who was sleeping by my feet. It was hard to believe I had another cat in my life. Fluffy had been always in my thoughts for all these years after he passed. And yes, then there was my husband, another person that didn't need to die, especially so young. It was truly hard to even think of anyone else after all these years.

I really didn't want to dwell too long on those thoughts. I had to think about David and finding a solution to what may have probably been a murder.

If Fred Stone heard me talking now, he would have been chewing my head off. I could hear him talking in my head.

"Mandy, there's no evidence, there's nothing there that says somebody came along and poisoned him. There were no prints on the glass, other than his own fingerprints. All the prints in that house, for the most part, were all David's. There was no evidence of violence. There was no evidence that anything suspicious had happened at all. It was all pure and simple suicide."

Suicide is never simple.

Maybe it will turn out that it was an accident. At least David's mother could feel better. And for that matter, I would too. The idea of David killing himself did not sit too well with me. I kept asking myself rhetorically, why David, why??? You had so much to live for. You could have come to me, I would have helped with whatever it was. You didn't have to die.

I still had to force myself to believe that David was gone. It felt like he had left on vacation, and he'd be back any moment to tell us all what a wonderful time he'd had in Saint Tropez, and then he'd ask us how his show went, if we'd gotten everything together in time.

And everything would go back to normal. But David was dead and no amount of wishful thinking would bring him back.

CHAPTER SIX

I sat at my desk going over the last-minute changes that Jill suggested we make to our page before submitting it to Bernard. The entrance to the gallery was wide and narrow. I stared out at it, waiting, though I didn't know what for. Perhaps I had hoped that someone would barge through the sunlit double doors and tell me that David was still alive.

The phone rang, startling me from my thoughts. It was Margot.

"Hi Mandy, David's service is going to be held tomorrow. It's a one day viewing."

I knew why. David's body hadn't been discovered until two days after his death, by the cleaning lady he hired to clean his apartment. I was certain that the mortician would have a hell of a time making David presentable. But those people were real artists and David would be viewable one way or another.

"Thanks for letting me know Margot. I'll be sure to let David's friends know where it is.

I'm just wondering if you might have found a list of

David's old clients?"

"Why is that important?"

"Well, I thought it would be nice if David's former clients could at least know that he has passed and get a chance to pay their respects. I'm sure that many became friends with David over the years and they would be happy to come. Some of them may even be thinking of doing work with him in the future and don't know he has recently passed."

Margot was quiet. Finally, she said, "ok."

This gave me an excuse to call Harold and tell him to invite whoever he could because they were having a funeral for David. Even though I had told Margot that I had contacted David's friends, I was really counting on Harold to come through with the actual contacts.

I had to move fast because I would only have one chance at the funeral, to talk to all the people that could possibly have killed David. Doing it this way would look less suspicious than if I was just calling people up here and there. If people wondered why I was asking so many questions, I would just say I'm just getting quotes and stories for David's memorial page. I had no idea who was going to show up, or if I was going to get the brush off from people. But it would give me a good collection people to at least talk to.

***

I was nervous about the meeting I would have with Bernard later that day regarding the page we had made for David.

I had seen Bernard earlier that afternoon. He had come to work is such a huff that when he passed me on his way to his office, all I caught was a blur of a brightly-patterned shirt and his brown trousers. Even his cane hit the ground with impatient thuds. He had slammed his office door and drawn the shade over the window so that no one could peer in. This behavior was usually an indicator that he was not to be bothered, which caused even more anxiety because I *had* to speak with him, and it could not wait until his mood had swung in another direction.

I was confident that Jill and Katie had done wonderful work on the page, and that most people would love what they had done. However, Bernard was in no way like most people. It was a total attitude crapshoot when it came to him.

The phone rang, and I swiveled my chair around to answer.

Jill's pleasant voice greeted me. "Hi, just wanted to let you know that I had time this morning to do additional work on the page. Check it out,"

I looked at the page and now it looked more professional. It gave me confidence to see how well it had turned out. I was glad she'd called- I was certain that Bernard would be sold on it. Still uneasy about meeting with the grump, but it was a confidence boot I needed.

When the time for the appointment with Bernard arrived, I went in his office and attempted small-talk, but Bernard was not one for chit-chat. He interrupted me before I could ask about his family, or the weather.

"So what do you have for me?" I went to his computer and brought up the page.

Bernard viewed the site, without uttering a sound, for an agonizing ten minutes while I observed from behind him.

"This page is very nice," Bernard said. I let out a long sigh. I hadn't realized that I'd been holding my breath. He seemed to enjoy all the mentions that we'd given the gallery, and he seemed happy with the overall aesthetic of the page.

"I'll be honest with you, I like the page, but I still don't see much value in doing the exhibit, I should really be focusing on bringing in someone new. People want to see the artist alive and if I showed the paintings, people would ask about the artist and there would be none to point the patron to."

I was a little angry and taken aback. David was my friend, but I understood that I could not look at this as a personal slight. It was a business proposition, and so I needed sell him on the business benefits.

"Well Bernard, maybe you're more used to dealing with tangible objects, but with social media, this page is just the beginning. If we did a memorial service at the gallery and showed the exhibit, we could film the whole thing and put it on YouTube and on Facebook. Afterwards, we could put up a couple of ads up on Facebook, aimed at people that like art and art galleries and these people would find it touching that the gallery did a service in honor of the recently deceased artist. They would be curious as to what other artists the gallery represents, and what other types of art we sell."

"So, you're saying it's a long-range project. People will discover the gallery and after seeing the David story, people would consider this place a more humane and artist friendly gallery?"

"That's one way of putting it, yes. and not only that, you could set the ads up to target only people who are interested in art galleries. That way, people interested in this sort of thing would become aware of the page and hopefully be interested in the visiting gallery, either in person or online."

"How much would this cost?" Bernard asked. I knew that was coming.

"I would pay for it, because I believe in David's art so much."

"No, no, you tell me how much you spent and maybe

we'll go halves, you're doing a lot of work for this exhibit as it is"

I omitted telling him that the ads were cheap and in the end, I didn't want to advertise the page. I just thought it was important to have a memorial at David's show. I just had to make it look that this would be great for the gallery. Plus I had also hoped that it would improve my chances of getting hired full time. That was another reason why I was taking such a serious interest in the welfare of the gallery.

Bernard hemmed and hawed for a little while longer.

"Okay, we'll do the art show and keep the pictures up for a couple of days. It will fill in the space while I look for someone else to exhibit. Hopefully the Facebook page will bring in people. By the way Mandy, I respect your dedication, if there's anything else you come up with talk to me, I'm sure we can work together to improve the gallery."

I could have jumped up and down, I was so excited, but I kept my cool, thanked Bernard, and told him he will be happy with the exposure that the gallery would receive.

***

After work, I ran home to spend time with Roger. I'd felt guilty that I had been so consumed with David that I'd not spent much time with my new cat. I needed a break from thinking about David. But was not allowed the opportunity, as I remembered that I needed to call Margot for David's client list.

I plucked my phone from the charger on my kitchen counter and dialed Margot's number.

She answered after the first ring.

"Hello Mandy. It's nice to hear from you again," Margot said. She sounded less hoarse than the last time we had spoken. I hoped she had been crying less.

"Hi Margot, I'm just wondering if by any chance you'd

found David's client list?

"Well, I found a folder with papers in it that looked like invoices and orders. I think that is probably it. Do you really think that his former clients are going to come?"

"I don't know, but there's no harm in trying. The worse they could say is no. I know that this is a sad occasion, but I think it can be made more special by inviting those that appreciated his work. It would show that he was loved. That he was not alone in the world"

"Thank you Mandy for helping out with this funeral. I'm not in the most social of moods and if it wasn't for my family helping, I don't know if many people would attend. I was in no state of mind to do what you've done for me. I doubt I could have called anyone."

"Oh, I completely understand, I'm doing this because I just believe that David was such a talented and special person that he deserves recognition in his farewell. How about I come by? I'll drop in to say hi for a moment, would that be okay?"

"Well of course it would, Mandy. I would appreciate some company," Margot said. We said goodbye to one another and hung up. I made sure to pet and feed Roger before I left. I hadn't planned on being gone very long, but I still left the television on for Roger.

***

When I arrived at Margot's house I found her down in spirits. She asked me if I wanted some coffee. We sat down at the kitchen table.

"My family has been really great setting up the arrangements so that I wouldn't have to. It's hard for a Mother to arrange her son's funeral."

And with this she started to cry. I cried too because this whole situation was just so sad. At that point Margot's sister, Nancy, who was visiting stepped into the room and started to comfort her.

"It's okay Margot, we're all here for you to support you if you need any help."

Nancy came over to me and introduced, "Hi, there, you must be Mandy. Margot has been telling me about you. Thank you for your help and your support for Margot."

"It my pleasure"

Margot remembered the client list I had come by to pick up.

"Mandy, this is all I was able to find, it looks like invoices and other papers. Hopefully, it's what you were looking for"

"Well, I won't know till I actually go through it, but there has to be some contact information for his clients."

Nancy came back and turned back to Margot. As I sat there, I felt that I was intruding upon family time, I figured it would be best if I left. I would have time with Margot when I helped her clean David's apartment.

"Margot, I'm going to be heading back now. Thanks for the client list,

With client list in hand, I left, hoping it would be more than a client list. I wanted to look at this to see if there wasn't anything fishy in here. Something, anything that would show there was something funny going on.

I got back to my house, and Roger was waiting for me when I opened the door. I wanted to bring him along for the ride before, but I didn't know what kind of situation I would encounter over at Margot's house. Even though I would have loved to have him with me, I was glad I left him home. It would have been awkward.

Roger already had a favorite toy, a stuffed banana with a little bell that he would hold in his paws and scratch and throw it and catch it. Maybe he liked the sound of the bell, but it was the toy that he paid the most attention to. I'm glad he was feeling at home and he was becoming more and more my cat. He was no longer an animal from the shelter. He was my cat.

As I watched him play, I still had to notice how big and muscular he was. He must be a mix of something other than tabby cause he was one big tabby. But for the most part he had a sweet face and looked like a grey tabby. Maybe he was a land of the giants kitten and would grow to be 7 feet tall. Somehow, I knew that was something I didn't have to worry about.

Even though, I was tired now that I was home, I was looking forward to exploring the client list. I grabbed my phone and my laptop and sat at my desk in the den.

Roger bounced happily behind me and curled up by my feet the moment I sat down.

I looked over the various client invoices. It seemed as though David had received deposits for various pictures. Maybe this wasn't the full client list. In any event, it was a start. Some of the invoices went back several months, one almost a full year. I made a neat pile of the invoices and started to call the numbers.

The first number I dialed was answered by a man. I felt a bit nervous, and was unsure of what to say. I hadn't actually thought that far into this. But that was just like me. I jumped head-first into so many situations. Maybe that's why I had so many jobs.

"Hello, may I speak to Timothy Landston?" I asked the man at the other end of the line.

"This is he, call me Tim"

"Hi, my name is Mandy Cummings. I'm calling because I have an invoice for one of the portraits that you had ordered from David Towsky six months ago, and I was wondering if you would like attend a service for David, since David had recently passed away."

There was a long silence on Tim's end. I was ready to ask if he was still on the line when he finally spoke.

"What?" Tim said. He sighed, was silent for another moment and then began to talk.

"Hi Mandy, I'm glad you called. Listen, let me tell you something. I've trying to get a hold of this David guy now for six months. Six months ago I ordered a portrait for my daughter that he said was going to be finished in one month. I paid a four hundred dollar deposit with a six hundred dollar balance to be paid when he delivered the picture. I never heard back from him. I would call and call and he never answered. I really thought that I had been swindled. How long was he in the hospital for?"

"Well, he wasn't in the hospital he died unexpectedly."

Tim huffed, and his voice grew louder so that I had to hold the phone further from my ear. Turning the volume down accomplished nothing.

"Well, I think I was right in my original assessment of the situation. I was going to cut him some slack because maybe he was sick but now you tell me he died unexpectedly which means that for six months this guy has been stringing me along. He took my four hundred dollars and I never got a picture. I reported him to the better business bureau and nothing ever came of it."

At this point, Tim switched from complaining to getting information.

"How are you related to him?"

"I'm just a friend. I have no idea of his business dealings. I was calling people at random that I thought he had done business with that might be interested in coming to the service. However, I can see that something happened here where you were not treated well. I will inform the person with power of attorney to look into this. Perhaps you can get a refund. I'm sorry, I'm just organizing the invitations for the service."

"Okay look, I won't chew your head off, but I really want my money back. Obviously this David guy never had the intention of making the portrait of my daughter. Please tell the people that handle this to give me a refund, since I paid a deposit and never got a picture. I never even got my daughter's picture back."

"I will. I'm truly sorry about this situation, hopefully they will find a way to fix this."

I hung up.

That was so strange. David squelched somebody for money? That was so unlike the David that I knew. But let's face it Mandy, you haven't dealt on a day to day basis with David in quite some time. Maybe Fred was right; we don't truly know the people we think we know.

I was amazed at what this man had said. He was pretty nice about it, all things considered. He could have been nastier.

I sifted through the remaining invoices- which were all similar. I found twenty total invoices that said David had gotten paid deposits up front- all the same number. Four hundred dollars. And they all had a balance of six hundred to be paid upon delivery. As far as I could tell, none had ever been delivered.

What had happened to David? This was not the David I knew. The David I knew would never rip people off. But I had proof. Fred had said that there was no evidence of a struggle. No evidence of foul-play. Only David's prints had been found on the glass. Could it be that David had gotten himself into so much debt that he thought that killing himself was the only answer?

I had a large file to sort through. I wondered what other secrets might be hiding within.

With the funeral two days away and the gallery memorial that weekend, there wasn't much time to delve into it. But I had to figure this out. Did David truly commit suicide and what my gut feeling was telling me is that he committed suicide for a reason, and here's one of the reasons? David had done something with that money, but what? Was he a drug addict?

I would have to reach out to Mike, the drug dealer that I went to high school with. Although he wasn't a drug dealer in high school, that's what he became and I hadn't associated with him for a long time, because of his activities. Yet, he was always friendly to me on the street, always said hi. It's not always good to still be in the minds of people you went to high school with.

I once did a reading for Mike when he came to some restaurant where I was working. He said he was doing it for fun. I think he liked me and he was trying to get close to me. But my wedding ring put him off, he said, *oh I didn't know you had gotten married*. Dumb he was not. But I guess that's how he survived as a drug dealer.

Now I wondered if perhaps I could ask him if David might have bought drugs from him. I could find out if David bought the pain killers for himself. And anything else he might have been on. He was taking all this money and not giving people their product. That sounds like he needed money for something. Like a drug habit.

I was growing upset and disappointed in David. I was beginning to feel as though I had been duped. Here I was going through this whole exercise of trying to preserve and honor David's memory. But what if David hadn't lived an honorable life?

He may have taken his life in order not to face whatever it was that he had done. Maybe he did something really rotten for no good reason other than selfishness or a drug induced spree. Well, I guess I would just have to keep on digging.

Maybe someone at the funeral home would know something. Maybe Harold would know something. It's possible Harold was trying to protect David's image knowing full well that David had been up to no good. Harold claimed that he cheated on David and that's why David broke up with him. But what if that wasn't the truth. What if David was just too far gone and Harold didn't want to stick around?

Harold was a good guy and that's just the sort of thing that he would do. Meanwhile, little naïve me was thinking bad thoughts about Harold because he was cheating on David. Well maybe David had been doing something that Harold wanted no part of. Well, I'm putting Harold on my list of people to talk to as soon as possible.

I would speak with Harold at the first opportunity.

In the course of all this, Roger had laid down next to me on the sofa and was resting his head on my thigh. He was purring. Maybe he could sense I was stressed out by all these new discoveries and needed some TLC. I looked at him, sprawled out on the sofa, his great length almost taking over the whole three quarters of the sofa. I'm glad that he was all my own.

Tomorrow would be another day and I'd grapple with what had been going on in David's life prior to him dying.

I got up from the sofa to make myself a cup of tea and Roger followed me into the kitchen. I opened a can of his favorite food and he dug into it like he hadn't been fed in months, even though it had been a couple of hours. I thought that all cats are were that way. Put some food in front of them and they'd eat as fast as possible in case it tried to disappear.

CHAPTER SEVEN

I was completely pre-occupied with what I had discovered the night before. All day I had felt as though I was in a fog. The night before I had a dream in which I was back in college and Daniel was alive and we were hanging out. And then David appeared completely strung out and acting a like a druggie. I asked him what happened and he said *Mandy, this is me, this is the real me.* I woke up in the middle of the night, sweating, Maybe it was my mind playing tricks on me.

I was imagining the worst, I was so shocked that David was ripping people off, it must have all gotten jumbled up and I went back to happier times but David himself wasn't happy. People usually kill themselves when they're not happy. More and more I thought maybe Fred had been right all along. But still, I had to finish this investigation for myself. I wanted to know what changes David had gone through over the last couple of years to become this David that I didn't know. A David that was ripping people off. Maybe Harold will shed more light into this.

I also had to find Mike, the drug dealer. I didn't have a number for him so I thought I would drive around town until I found him somewhere. I also didn't know what to expect. I hadn't had communications in years with this guy and who knows if he was dangerous now. Maybe I was getting in over my head and I should just leave this alone, tell Fred of the non delivered portraits and let the police handle it. They would find an answer.

Still I didn't want Mike to be hassled by the police because I had an idea about something that may be totally off the mark. There was me again, always trying to make nice to everybody. I had been like this in high school and I had been a door mat for so many people cause I was always trying to please everybody and trying be nice when people were just taking advantage of me. And here I was again, hoping that I didn't get somebody in trouble. That it would be my fault. This was a drug dealer were talking about. He'd been nice to me, but had he been so nice to everybody? Who knows?

The day finally came to an end and I decided I would try to find Mike. I took Roger with me. I didn't want to go alone. After driving around for an hour, I found him parked near the mall, leaning up against his car. Maybe he was waiting for a customer. Maybe he was just hanging out. Whatever it was, this was my chance to talk to this guy.

I parked my car behind his and got out with Roger. Mike spoke first.

"Mandy! Don't' tell me that you've come to buy drugs. I am going to be soooo disappointed. If ever there was somebody I thought that was going to be nice for the rest of her life it was you. You're not going down the dark path now are you?"

He smiled while he spoke, then let out a loud guffaw.

"I see that you brought your attack cat with you. I heard about the guy in the mall. A lot of creeps have been coming around these parts lately. Good thing you had a cat to help you out of danger. This one sounds like a real champ. How can I help you?"

"Well Mike, you'll pardon my intruding into your life — "

"Intruding, you're never intruding Mandy."

"Well, I have to ask you a sensitive question. Believe me, this is just between you and me. I just have to find this out for my peace of mind. There are no cops involved, I just can't believe what happened to a friend of mine. It's looking more and more like he was not the person I thought he was and I just need to know if he ever bought drugs from you?"

"Whoa Mandy, I can't give that kind of information. I have trust with my customers and if I rat them out, well they don't come back, see, it's bad for business, so as much as I like you, I can't tell you stuff like that."

"Listen Mike, if it's losing business you're worried about, don't worry, this guy is dead and that's my dilemma. You see, the police say it's suicide and I knew he was allergic to a certain type of drug that is popular, and he died of that drug. I just need you to look at his picture and tell me if he ever bought drugs from you. It's just so I can resolve this in my head. If he did, then I'll accept he did kill himself and that's that."

"Well, in that case, if the guy's already dead, but you gotta understand I can't answer much, I'll just see if I know him, let me look."

Mike took a look at David's picture.

"Oh yeah, this guy was a real pothead, he bought a lot of pot from me but that was it. I never heard of anybody dying from pot."

"No, it's not pot he died of, he died from an opioid pain killer."

"Well, I never sold him that. That's not to say that he

didn't buy it from somebody else. I wish I could help you but that's all I know on him."

I felt defeated and at the same time, sad to know that David had gone down this route. Maybe all that money was to support a pot habit?

"Well, thanks Mike, at least it does explain some things about him. I appreciate you sharing that with me. I won't tell a soul."

"No problem Mandy, sorry to hear about your friend. I could see that you're disappointed about your friend. Good old Mandy, always the good girl. Some people we don't really know, Mandy. Your friend could have been putting on an act."

"I'm beginning to think you're right. One last question Mike, and I understand if you won't tell me. Did anybody else recently buy opioid pain killers from you."

Mike looked pensive and said, "I don't know Mandy, I don't know if I could say that. It just puts me in a bind."

"Mike you don't have to tell me who they are, just if somebody did."

"I don't know Mandy, I get paranoid about questions like that."

"It's ok Mike, I understand. Thanks, you've been very helpful, I appreciate it."

I walked back to my car with Roger. I was sat in silent contemplation for a couple of seconds. David a pothead. Then, all of a sudden, there was a violent banging on my window. It startled me out of my mood. I looked through my left window, and there was Mike motioning to roll down the window. What now, I thought?

"Listen Mandy, I'm going to say this, but you never mention this to anybody, ok? Two guys bought the painkillers from me, one regular and another one I've never seen before. That's all I got don't ever ask me any more questions about my clients."

"Thank you Mike. I'll never tell a soul."

I drove off thinking about what Mike had just said - one a regular customer, another buyer a guy he never dealt with before. Could somebody have bought the opioid pain killer to kill David? Was this payback for a deal gone sour? It seemed that as far as his art was concerned, David had done a couple of sour deals.

Whoever it was, it had to be somebody that knew he was allergic to this substance, drugged his water, and left afterwards. David just drank the water, maybe being stoned out of his mind and then had the allergic reaction, couldn't breathe and just died in his bed. But what could have been the motive? This I was going to have to figure out. Maybe there were more clues in that envelope that I got from Margot.

Whereas before I didn't think that anybody would want to kill David, I was beginning to believe that maybe more than one person had a reason to kill David, even it was over something trivial. He just got involved with somebody nuts enough to kill him for whatever it was. That's all it took these days, one crazy person who had a bad day and decided that the only way to right a wrong is by killing the person who did you wrong.

But it had to be someone close, someone that knew that David had an allergy to opioid pain killers. Harold was such a person. Could Harold have done it? Maybe David did something terrible to Harold and this was one of those crimes of passion. Had I been living in a fog all these years while the world around me was going crazy?? Maybe I had been so caught in the in the grief of losing my mother, my cat and my husband that I didn't pay too much attention to the rest of the world.

It was hard to think of my old friends as anything other than the icons I had made them out to be. In my head, they were all just as simple to understand as I was to myself. But I was slowly learning that this was not the case. Some people had changed for the better while others had changed for the worse. And maybe David had been one of those who had taken a turn for the worse.

I was upset about what I had learned from Mike. I needed to speak to Harold. Harold may not be entirely forthcoming with what he knew too. Maybe he was trying to protect David. Or himself. I pulled into Joanie's Cupcakes and called Harold.

"Hi Harold I'm at Joanie's you want to meet me here? I'd love to hear about who you might have recommended and who will be coming to the funeral."

I was being fake nice, sounding chirpy as though I was an events planner who was helping plan this funeral. Truth to tell, it wasn't far from it. Originally I had done it to find out if anybody had a motive to kill David. Now I was beginning to think that maybe David drove them to it.

I took Roger out of the car with his leash on. I knew that Joanie would love to see Roger again, she was a cat lover too. Many a time I had brought Fluffy to her place with the collar so she was used to me bring my cat around everywhere regularly.

"Oh you're bringing this beautiful baby here again? Hi Roger, you're a beautiful boy." Joanie said.

She brought him a saucer of milk, which Roger devoured. Well, Roger had another fan. He drank his milk and then sat down, tucking his paws under him, the "hen keeping her eggs warm" pose that all cats do at some point or another. And here was Roger doing his version of that. It must be an instinctual thing because all cats do it. .

The bell at the shop door rang, and in came Harold. He flashed his very white teeth at me in what appeared to be a genuine smile. In his hand, he held a few pieces of paper that had been paperclipped together. He settled into the booth on the opposite side of me and slid the sheets of paper across the table.

"I managed to get a hold of all these people. All are okay with you asking them questions. However, there was this particularly nasty guy who always envied David and him and David were having a feud for the longest time because David was always undercutting him in price for portraits."

That allowed me to jump in.

"Listen Harold, I want you to be honest with me. You know we're friends and as friends we're doing all we can to honor David's memory. Whatever I ask is between you and me and I'm not going to go to the police with this. I need to know for my own peace of mind."

Harold looked at me like I had two heads.

"What happened, what are you talking about?"

"Ok, it's this. I got a folder of invoices from Margot. I thought it would be a good idea to call some past clients as they might want to go to the wake. However, I called the first one and he was kind of angry because he had paid David a deposit of four hundred dollars and David never delivered the picture. I was lucky the guy didn't go off on me. However, looking through the rest of the invoices, he had twenty of the same type of invoices. He took a deposit and never delivered the pictures."

Harold was a little taken aback and at the same time, thought about events that happened back then.

"Wow, I knew he was getting some money here and there around the time we had broken up, but it wasn't amazing money. I figured he was doing jobs, I never asked him when he was working. But I didn't know he was taking money from people and not delivering. That isn't like David. There's gotta be more to this."

"I didn't want to believe it, either, but I looked through this folder and there were twenty people with the same situation as the guy I spoke to. So, either David was losing his mind, or David was not really showing his true colors to us. Maybe he was going through a difficult period."

"Well, he was acting a little strange. I think that's why I cheated on him, I really didn't want to be around him, he wasn't that much fun anymore. Maybe I could have helped him more, but he never came to me with any concerns. He never told me he'd felt different, or terrible. He kept it all hidden.

More and more it looked like David was leading a double life. He needed money for pot, and maybe for other drugs, and he wasn't doing work. Maybe he was depressed. He should have reached out to friends. There you go again Mandy, thinking of shoulda, coulda, but the fact is, David's dead and that's not going to bring him back.

I had been wrong to ever classify David as a deadbeat. He wasn't. He was emotionally disturbed.

"So Harold, from what you saw, was David doing the pot for medicinal reason?"

"Nah, he was just becoming a pot head. Honestly, I think part of the reason I cheated on him was that he just wasn't the old David I knew, he was going on a weird direction and maybe that's what turned away from him. He was not the fun guy I originally met. Mandy, there were screws in there that were becoming loose and looking back now, maybe he needed therapy and he never sought it out.

"He just went in some weird direction where he kept making wrong decisions. There was also talk, although who knows if this was true, that he had some kind of secret lover. I never found out if this was true, or if this was something he was telling me just to get revenge.

Something immature, I have a secret lover. Yeah right. I mean, for instance, I got a new lover but people saw us together quite a bit. I never saw David with anybody. Which tells me that was just something he was telling me to try to get me jealous. I won't take you back cause now I have a secret lover. Like a kid. Na na, I got a boyfriend and I won't be your boyfriend."

Harold said this in a sing songy style

After speaking with Harold, I was just as much in the dark as I had been before.

David seemed to be relying on pot and who knows what else to deal with the realities of life. Not that it mattered now because he was dead. I had to keep reminding myself. I would go off in these tangents in my mind, where I wanted to talk to him and say, David you have to give back that money, you went about this whole thing the wrong way. But there was no David to scold. David was dead.

CHAPTER EIGHT

The day of the funeral I woke up early, not having been able to sleep well. I had a lot of things on my mind and the discoveries of the last couple of days had kept me awake. Roger rubbed himself against my legs as I walked. I figured I'd better feed him before I became distracted.

However, it's hard to forget to feed a hungry cat. They have ways of reminding you and if they don't get you the first time, the second, third, fourth or fifth reminder will alert you to the fact that you haven't fed them. Cats are good like that. For me, it was just great to have a kitty in the house and Roger was turning out to be a very affectionate cat with very little maintenance.

Before heading to work, I got all my information in order. I had all the names of people that Harold had contacted. They said it was okay for me to reach out to them about David, including the Nasty guy. Although I didn't look forward to any confrontations, maybe this nasty guy had something serious against David. Maybe it was more than just rivalry. Maybe David had done something underhanded to him and he was still angry about it.

I went on Facebook to see what these people looked like. I couldn't possibly remember everybody but I figured Harold would fill me in on who I had missed.

So far, my "investigation", if you could call it that, had turned up things that weren't very flattering about David and basically, showed him in a way that I would never imagine David to be. Maybe one of these people could shed a little light as to what happened to David.

Also, I might learn if there really had been a secret boyfriend or that was just a ruse, as Harold said, to make Harold jealous. This certainly was not the job I had signed up for. I just wanted to do something to remember my friend, something that would have had positive impact on his legacy. And to prove to myself that he didn't commit suicide, that this whole suicide thing was a mistake that I was sure I could clear up. Now, I wasn't so sure. I hated uncertainty, and I just didn't know what was going on.

Jill called to ask if I had any more material for the fan page. I told her maybe after the funeral, the former clients were a no go and that I would tell her the story later, while I was at work. I told Bernard that the funeral was today and he said that he might not be able to make it because of some prior engagements. That sounded like a poor excuse to me, but I didn't want to push it since he had agreed to do the showing and to give a brief memorial presentation. You have to pick your battles.

Besides, the funeral had taken on a whole new meaning to me. I had to see if any of the people attending could have been someone that wanted David dead. Or could shed some light on why he had taken his life. Somebody knew something, that although might be a mystery to me, it might not have been a mystery to others that dealt with him on a regular basis.

***

I left work at noon and headed for the funeral parlor.

This was one of the newer funeral homes. The layout was very clean and minimal. First person I saw when I got there was Margot and gave her a hug. Apart from three or four mourners, I didn't recognize the rest of the people. The majority of those assembled so far were David's distant relatives that had come into town, whom I had never met. Harold had told me he'd be there at one in the afternoon and that the people he invited would trickle in, there was no time set. It was looking like a long day in the funeral parlor if I wanted to talk to as many people as possible. I told myself that if nothing came out of all of this, at least I had closure in that I did the right thing. Maybe it would always be a mystery as to what happened to David.

I was relieved to see Harold when he arrived. I was much more comfortable to be with a person that I knew well.

"Mandy, it's creepy here. I can't go near that casket. I'll stay with you. Ask me about anyone. I'll tell you what I know," he said.

He looked like he didn't want to be there, but felt obligated to. This was harder for him than I had realized. But like me, I think he was beginning to want some answers. Things weren't as cut and dry as they seemed to be just 3 days ago.

I spoke to some people I knew and they all spoke of how surprised they were to hear that David to had committed suicide, they had read the news and that's how they learned about his passing. Inasmuch as the term suicide still didn't sit well with me, I thanked them for coming to the funeral and went on to talk to the next person. The next person I spoke to that Harold had recommended was a guy by the name of Michael Chalmers.

I introduced myself and he recognized my name as the one that Harold gave him. I proceeded to ask my first question.

"So, how long did you know David for?"

"Oh, I've known him since high school. We were pretty close and as far as I can remember, David was always talking about his art. Once he went to college, I lost contact with him for a while. He came back, and I tried to be friendly. He was friendly as well, and we would have some chats here and there, but nothing beyond that. A couple of weeks ago, he told me he had discovered a creative way of making money, which would allow him to pursue his more artsy ambitions. I also learned from him about this upcoming art show he was doing. He mentioned that even though he viewed his portrait work as his bread and butter, he figured that all artists have a secret longing to do artsy stuff, artsy being different depending on who you spoke with."

I thanked him and I asked myself what David could have meant by the word "creative". Taking people's money was not creative, it was devious and dishonest.

I spoke to a couple of other people during the course of the afternoon and they offered fluff - they didn't really know David.

Then I ran across another person Harold had recommended, Trevor. I recognized him from his Facebook picture.

"Hi, I'm Mandy Cummings, Harold had said you might be stopping by."

"Oh yes, Harold had mentioned that you would be asking some questions about David. I have to say, I was very surprised that Harold was involved with anything relating to the funeral."

"Why is that?"

"Well, apparently, David dumped Harold in a really lousy way, telling him that they were over and that he was seeing someone else. I remember running into Harold that day and he was very hurt and angry. He was saying that he was going to get even with David for what he did, that he wasn't going to stand for anybody using him and throwing him away, like a tissue. I didn't pay it much mind, I figured they had a lover's quarrel and all would be well in no time. I loved David as a friend, even though he seemed a little weird lately. But you know, he was an artist, and artists have these weird episodes in their life. Look at Vincent VanGogh. He cut off his ear for the love of a prostitute. David wasn't that weird, but now that he committed suicide, honestly I wished he would have cut off an ear for Harold. At least he would still be with us. Excuse me, I just have to see my other friend over there."

That revelation was like a bucket of cold water. Why hadn't Harold told me the truth? Did he want to divert attention from himself as to why David died? He had left early and said he felt creepy being there. Was it guilt?? Could he have had anything to do with David's death?? This was just getting more and more insane.

The day was getting long. There's only so much time you could spend at a funeral. But I had to stay if I wanted answers. So far, it had been fruitful. More people showed up over the next couple of hours, but most just paid their respects.

Then there was another person I recognized from his web page. Jake, another artist. As I went up to him and said hi, I suddenly remembered who he was. This was the nasty guy. I had no graceful way to step away.

"Oh yes, Harold told me that you might approach me about David. Listen if you're looking for good news about David, I'm not the one to ask."

"I'd love to hear everyone's viewpoints good and bad, but could we step outside? There's family here and sometimes they're touchy when it's not praise for the dead family member."

He looked around and huffed but reluctantly agreed. We exited the funeral parlor and stood on the sidewalk outside.

"Let me tell you off the bat, that me and David have always been rivals. At first it had been friendly rivalry but as the years went by, David kept undercutting me in prices and taking business away."

"Well, that doesn't sound so horrible, people are always trying to get business and unfortunately cutting prices is a common practice."

"Well, I was particularly angry at him for the last six months. Apparently David had really been aggressive about getting clients and he had taken on all these customers. A couple of dozen. I was asking myself, is David a superman, he's going to do all these portraits in a month's time? I smelled a rat. You know what that little creep was doing? He was outsourcing the portraits and putting his name on them. I couldn't figure it out at first how someone could do so many portraits and some of them pretty good. But after looking at some of them I could see that they were in different styles. One person had not done all those portraits.

"I know because being sneaky like I am, I asked those clients to see his work, as a way of getting business in the future. I started to follow David. I was basically stalking him. He would go to different clients' homes and get their business, then I would follow him all the way from the client's house till he got home. Once home, I would look through his window. It wasn't easy, but I wanted to see what he was doing. I would see him scanning the picture. Now if he did this only once I wouldn't have thought twice about it. But all the time I was spying on him, he was only doing his own paintings, not portraits. Four or five times I followed him for the portrait business, I would never see him start a portrait, only scan pictures he got from the clients and continue doing his own paintings.

"I couldn't figure it out at first but then it hit me, he was outsourcing. Looking up online painters, I found one service that if you sent them a picture they would do a hand drawn oil paint for $150 bucks. That's how he was undercutting me. And that's how he found time to do his paintings for his show."

"Do you have proof of this", I asked.

"I don't have hard evidence that I could show you, I just stalked him and looked through his windows. Yes, I know it sounds sad and pathetic, but when somebody is taking food from your mouth, you want to find out how they're doing it. Recently, as I was trying to get new business, I found out that he wasn't even bothering to do the work he was hired for.

"He was taking people's deposits and not delivering the paintings. And the reason I know this is because I got two jobs where they asked me if I knew a David Towsky because they had given him a deposit for a painting and he disappeared. I said I didn't know him. I also told them I would never do such a thing and that I would contact them as soon as I had the picture ready, or they could come by my house if they wanted to check up on me and see the progress.

"So, not only had he stolen business from me, now he had created distrust in the community. My guess is that his Chinese connection went out of business, he spent the money, and didn't bother to contact the people that hired him for the portraits. So, that's your little friend David, a crook, a cheat and a liar. Maybe he got what he deserved, or he killed himself because he couldn't live with himself anymore. You can close your mouth now."

And he stalked off.

It was true that while he was telling me all of this, I was dumbfounded. He had figured it out. That explained all those invoices that David had. If I looked further in that folder, I bet I would find the orders to whoever it was he was outsourcing work to.

I could also see that this guy had it in for David, even if David had never done anything wrong. He was jealous and he was a very unhappy person. But he also was trying to protect his turf in a desperate way. It also explained why David hadn't delivered the paintings. But he should have given refunds. He had probably spent the money. The whole thing was such a mess.

I felt terrible for Margot because as executor of the state and power of attorney, all those problems could come to haunt her. I would have to tell her at some point so she wasn't blindsided. It's hard enough to learn that your son had committed suicide, it was doubly hard to learn that a son you loved was doing all these shady things on the side.

Now she would have to right those wrongs or be open to lawsuits from all these people. Sooner or later somebody would read the news and come forward asking for reparations. They may think their calls weren't returned cause the artist died, but when they learn that the artist died recently, they're going to ask, why didn't he return our calls a couple of months back. I couldn't take it any longer, I had to get out of there. I went back into the funeral home and bid goodbye to Margot, told her I would call her the next day. I had to get some air and get a coffee or something to calm my nerves. That conversation with Jake had rattled me. I called Jill and told her to meet me at Joanie's in a half hour. Before heading out to Joanie's, I stopped by my house to feed Roger. I had left him plenty of food at noon and by now it was time for a second feeding. After he had eaten his dinner, I put the collar on him and went down to Joanie's to meet Jill.

Jill saw Roger from a distance

"There's that beautiful grey tabby." She petted him and rubbed him under his chin.

"He looks very relaxed and well fed. This cat is a perfect fit for you. Look, he doesn't even try to run away from strangers. . So, did you learn anything at the funeral?"

"Well, things are getting weirder and weirder. Harold contacted all these people that I talked to regarding David. He truly did come through in that capacity. He said he wanted to do everything he could to help me out. However, when he got to the funeral home, he was getting very nervous and saying that it was creeping him out to go near the corpse. He had a very scared look about him "

"Creeping him out?? That's strange"

"Right, but I let it go. Here's what made it even weirder, he left shortly after I got there. I thought I would have had someone there that I could talk to without having to put on an act and he skips out on me. So, that's the first thing that was weird. Second thing, I talked to a guy who was a mutual friend of David and Harold. Get this, he said that David dumped Harold, very ungraciously, and that Harold was extremely hurt and angry and that he was going to get revenge. What exactly does that mean?"

Jill looked astonished at learning these news.

"Yeah, that doesn't sound good. I truly hope that Harold didn't do something stupid. Maybe he just meant to hurt him so, but it turned into something bigger and he killed him accidentally?"

"That's what I thought too. What started out as just hurting him, wound up killing him instead. But wait, it gets even worse. I talked to this other guy, Jake, that was supposedly very nasty and he lived up to his reputation."

I told Jill of the exchange I had with Jake and she was flabbergasted. It wasn't so bad that David had outsourced his work, but the fact that he had taken people's money and didn't give it back was what upset Jill the most.

Jill said, "But why would he do such a thing? David has

always been so nice. It's very disconcerting hearing these things. As far Harold is concerned, it's definitely strange behavior for somebody who just the other day was being very helpful and cooperative in putting you in contact with people to share their stories about David."

Mandy shared her view.

"I was thinking it's possible, if Harold did kill David, that whatever he had done wasn't real to him until he saw David dead and now he was freaking out cause he thought he was going to get caught. I'm going to have to speak to Harold again but be very careful I don't let on I suspect him, because he could just run away before he could be brought to justice."

"It's crazy, one moment, I'm thinking that perhaps David had gotten into something very bad, the next, it's possible that Harold killed him over jealousy or hurt pride. I mean, how many people knew that David had this painkiller allergy? Very few. But Harold was among them."

Jill said, "I didn't know, so that shows you it was a very select group. Whoever killed him was somebody that knew personal things about David."

"As much as I hate to think so, it could have been Harold."

Roger leapt onto my lap, as if he could sense that I'd become disappointed in humanity and wanted to provide me comfort. Sure, humans were terrible, but cats, well, they at least give cuddles when you're down. Between Jake's rant and Harold acting strange, I wasn't feeling very warm and fuzzy. But Roger sat on my lap and purred. I was so glad at that moment that I found him. He was the perfect cat.

CHAPTER NINE

After I got home that night, I started work on my Powerpoint presentation for the gallery memorial. I had started this whole process, and I had to finish it, in spite of what I had learned thus far. No good deed goes unpunished. I don't know that I would have been so motivated for this memorial had I known what I knew now. But more and more it, looked like somebody had murdered David and it looked like it was somebody close to him. I was so hoping that it wasn't Harold, but there were few suspects to pick from. Unless Jake was dead set in killing David and knew about his allergy, I really couldn't think of anybody else.

I was angry that I couldn't go to Fred with what I'd discovered. He would just say that the case was closed. There was no evidence. I could tell him about David's unethical business practices and Fred probably wouldn't be bothered by it. He sees much worse on an hourly basis.

I wanted to consult my tarot cards, but I was not in a good state of mind. The cards worked best when the user was in a calm state, and I was far from calm.

I decided that the best way to calm down was to focus on the Gallery and not on David. I thought it would be best to focus on how even though I had introduced David to Bernard, that it was Bernard's vision to exhibit David's paintings, he had been so impressed by them. At the very least, my presentation could bolster my chances of getting hired in full time at the gallery. It was a struggle to think of nice things to say about David. I thought instead about the nice things about the gallery- mostly I thought of the lovely artwork, which I was sure anyone could appreciate.

I originally told Bernard that this was going to be helpful to the gallery so, writing it from this angle I was not lying. I knew that Bernard would be pleased. And it took my mind off some of the day's events.

I figured I could give my work to Katie in the morning and she would make sure that the slide show worked. She was going to play the slide monitor, so she would move the slides. It wasn't going to be long, so it was easy to put together. After I finished this, I figured I'd watch tv to take my mind off things.

This was also an excellent way to introduce Roger to my favorite shows. I'm sure that cats don't watch television, but they sit by your side and while you're watching tv. So for all intents and purposes they are watching tv with you. Roger laid on the sofa with his head on my lap and looked at the tv. It must be sights and sounds that keep them fixed on watching tv. But in my head, I always told myself that the cat was watching tv with me. Fluffy always did this and now the role was filled by Roger. Every once in a while I would have a slight pang of guilt about getting Roger and I would remember what Jill said that Fluffy was looking down on me wishing for my happiness. I would do the same for Fluffy if it was the reverse. Besides I hadn't replaced Fluffy. I was just expanding the number of cats in my life.

***

The next morning I took Roger with me to work. People bring their kids to work, right? Roger was the closest thing to me. Everybody was very happy to see him and a lot of people came over to my desk to pet him and inquire about him, the usual activity when you bring a kid or a pet to work. I was amazed to see that Roger just sat next to me and if people pet him or talked about him he stayed calm. There was no trepidation or hissing at strangers

My coworkers were just as shocked as I was to learn that Roger could use a toilet. Like a human. He even flushed. I had noticed that I hadn't needed to clean his litterbox often, but it never occurred to me until that day at the gallery that Roger had been doing his business like a person would.

I wondered how his previous owner had trained him to do that. I also wished I could have thought of it when I had Fluffy.

I also hoped I could train him to go during our walks. I planned on simply picking up after him like I would a dog.

I gave the file to Katie and she said the slides worked well. The animation didn't get stuck anywhere. She saw some of the text and snickered, "Trying to suck up to the boss, aren't we?"

"It's a long story and believe me, once this is over, I'll tell you everything and you'll understand why."

Shortly after that I asked Bernard if I could show him my presentation. He said sure come on in.

I gave a little background on the file, "I tried to give a balanced view of the gallery as it interacts with the artists and also you as director. I figured, when people watched the video, it would give them more of a reason to visit in the future."

As he watched, he saw that the presentation was about the paintings, and the that it heavily flattered the gallery. I also wrote about the gallery's history with local artists and how Bernard always had the vision for local talent and I linked that vision to the discovery of David's work.

"You know, at first I thought that all you were going to do was write about David, because he was your friend, but this is very objective. You've included David, but also the gallery and its history. Very nice."

I thought it was going to be cheesy, but Bernard ate it up. All through the presentation, he gave the thumbs-up sign as some slide went by, and he smiled a lot. When it was finished, he said -

"This was much different than what I was expecting. Thank you very much, I can see that you have absorbed the culture of the gallery in your time here. Let me know if there's anything you need me to do for this presentation, I'd be glad to.

"I have to be honest, if it wasn't for you initiating this whole memorial, I never would have done it and just moved on. However seeing everything you've done, it's opened my mind about possibilities of promoting the gallery in the future. I'm just old school and never think much about modern ways of getting the word out. This is a great beginning."

"Well, I'm glad that you enjoyed it, here's to more shows in the future."

I didn't want to tell Bernard that I'd had a change of heart about David. That wouldn't have gone over very well. But hey, I started this whole project, and I was going to finish it in a way that worked for everybody. We all were going to have to come back to work after this show and start setting up for the next art show, for whoever and whenever that was going to be. Life would go on. Only a few people, like myself, would remember David. Like so many others before him, he would continue to live the minds and hearts of those who loved him.

These shows were the lifeblood of the gallery and as long as there was as a show, there would be patrons and that usually translated into dollars at some point. It also provided jobs for people like me and others around me. I knew the gallery was like a hobby for Bernard, but still he tried to make it look like a business venture and he had to make money doing it.

If he was faking it, he sure was doing a good job. But it didn't matter to me. I had a job, the place was a nice place to work and I liked the people. There aren't a lot of places you could say that about. And it was possible that this was going to turn into a permanent job.

***

I called Margot to remind her that whenever she was ready to start packing David's things, I would be there to help her. Inasmuch as now I was doing it more for her than David. She knew nothing about the things I had discovered, and I knew that this was a very painful time for her. At some point I would have to tell her about some of things that David had done. But not right now. It could wait.

We could empty out David's apartment first and I would eventually tell her. It wasn't like there any pending lawsuits, just a lot of disgruntled people who gave up. Apparently if they can afford to pay for a portrait, maybe four hundred dollars is not a lot of money to them. Still, no matter what the amount, it's the way things were done. Not ethical business practices. There you go again Mandy, being miss goody two shoes. When was I finally going to stop doing this? Still, Margot had to know so it wouldn't bite her in the rear when she least expected it. I owed her at least that much.

The next day, I met Margot at David's apartment. When you walked in, the place was very still and for all intents and purposes, it looked like a regular apartment. There was no air of death there. It was as though David had stepped out and we were just waiting for him to come back. Except he was never coming back. Not now, not ever. Margot had gotten a lot of disassembled boxes. She said she was going to put everything in storage until she could figure out what to do with David's things. She to vacate the apartment, before it was put it up for rent again. She could have kept paying the rent but putting things in storage was cheaper. Not that anybody in her family was going to live in that apartment.

She looked around and said, "You know, it's strange when you have to bury your own son. Not because he was sick, not because he was in an accident but because he took his own life. I've asked myself in the last couple of days was it something that I didn't do, that I didn't instill in him as far as valuing himself? I always accepted him for who he was, I never once stopped supporting him, if he was happy the way he was, that's all that mattered to me. And he was talented too. He had so much to live for and yet, here I am, emptying out his apartment because he killed himself. Not what a mother ever envisions herself doing. You envision graduations, marriages, grandchildren. Not a dead son."

My heart went out to her. I felt terrible and at the same time I didn't dare tell her any of the things I'd discovered in the past couple of days. In the near future, I'd let her know.

I said, "You know Margot, let's not go too crazy here today. You tell me how long you want to stay and we'll pack whatever we can in that time. It's not like this is a race, nor do we have to do this in a short time frame. This is a horrible situation and I think you're very brave for tackling it. I won't leave you alone, I'll be right here. Don't come here by yourself, we'll do this together"

She gave me a hug and even though she had cried some, I could see that she was grateful for the help. We each grabbed boxes and set to work. After a couple of hours, I had put away at least four boxes of knick knacks and kitchen utensils.

At one point, I went into the bedroom, which I was avoiding, since that's where David had died. I saw David's collection of stuffed animals. He had them all arranged on either side of the bed, on love seats. All kinds and all sizes. I could see that in some ways he had never grown up. He was still holding on to his toy animals like some kind of safety net to adulthood.

As I looked around all the different types of animals, one thing stuck out. There were dozens of stuffed animals all around the bed. However, there was one lonely teddy bear on a shelf across the bed. I went to take a closer look to see if this was what I thought it was. I squeezed the bear and felt a hard spot in the front. It was a nanny cam. Then it dawned on me. David was filming his romps with his lovers. Well, I guess different strokes for different folks. Fred was right. You just didn't know the people you think you knew.

Then it came to me. What if there was video there of David's last hours? What if this thing had been on? What if it was filming and caught something that wasn't supposed to happen? I had to get this bear out of here and not raise any suspicion on Margot's behalf. I asked, "Margot, is it ok if I keep one of David's stuffed animals. I just want something to remember him by." She said, "Of course Mandy, take whatever you like." I took the bear and put it in my bag.

After three more hours of putting things away in the apartment, I asked Margot

"You think we've done enough for today?"

"I think we did a lot of good work, this was a good first step."

We had packed about twelve boxes. David, like many artists, was a minimalist, and other than the stuffed animals, he decorated well but sparsely. There wasn't much furniture for us to pack, which was a good thing because Margot wasn't in peak physical health.

Margot and I went to Joanie's for a bite to eat once we had finished at David's. After we'd sat down at the counter, I decided to tell Margot about some of the new people I'd met at the funeral.

"You know Margot, I sent out a lot of invitations for the funeral and a lot of people showed up. Just shows you, a lot of people loved David and were truly sad to see him go."

I was really surprised at the turnout. Thank you for inviting all those people. It made me feel less alone in this whole process, that other people were grieving too. I guess misery loves company, but it was nice to see all of those people.

I really appreciated that you stayed as long as you did talking to the guests. That took a burden from me. I wasn't in a chatty mood, and I saw that you talked to a lot of people"

I said "anytime", although, the truth was I was there for an ulterior motive. No matter how things turned out, at least Margot and I would have a good, strong friendship.

Roger was waiting for me to feed him the moment I walked through the front door. He was happy to see me, which made me feel great. That wonderful feeling of being greeted by your cat when you get home. I sat and rested with him seated next to me on the sofa. I had to be honest with myself, it was very hard to have spent time in David's apartment. Aside from everything I had learned about him, it was still hard knowing that I had been in the same place where a human being had recently died of unnatural causes. It just puts you in a distraught frame of mind.

Right now I was just chilling out, my cat was purring

on my lap, I was drinking a cup of coffee. Day after tomorrow was going to be David's memorial at the gallery. Once that was over I could go back and relax. I had tried to get answers for my own peace of mind about David and instead, learned a lot of things I really never wanted to know. It changed my opinion of him. It made me feel bad for him. There was still that question of whether Harold was ultimately responsible for what happened and he had been running scared all this time, hoping nobody would find out.

A number of people were acting strange since David's death and any one of them could have killed David. Or maybe no one but David was responsible for his own death. In the end, I may just have to go with the original results of the police: this was a suicide.

Roger got off my lap and started to play with one of his toys. He would slap it around with his paws and walk almost on his hind legs, he was so excited. It was great having a cat in the house again. I could see that over the years this was going to bring me hours of happiness just seeing him at play and taking him for walks around town and the happiness you can only get from a cat. Most people don't understand this, but animal people know this very well.

No matter what your pet of choice is, there is a love you get from an animal that you're not going to get from any human being on this earth. In many ways, animals are more advanced than we are. For all our intellect, we systematically hurt each other on purpose. Animals would never do that. They might hunt for food, or fight to protect themselves, but not for fun or to harm others. Those "hating for fun" activities are qualities that are uniquely human. While I was thinking all this heady stuff, Roger brought his toy over to me so that I could play with him. It's kitty play time.

CHAPTER TEN

After dinner I decided to explore the teddy bear I had taken from David's apartment. I was certain that it was a nanny cam, but hopefully one of the self contained ones, not the ones that transmit the video to a remote server. I was in luck, this one had a camera and a SD card to dump the video to. This is exactly what I was hoping for. I was sure that David would from time to time, take out the SD card, copy the files to his computer and watch. Well, to each their own, I guess.

For David, love must have been better the second time around. I asked myself, how much stuff was in here, had it been turned on when he took his life and what else was I going to find here? Well, if there was any footage of what happened the day David died, it might be here. I copied all the files to my computer, and started to look at the videos.

They had weird number codes and for some reason the dates were all the same. The manufacturers probably didn't put high quality cameras in these devices. David most likely hadn't cared about the exact date. He would just take it out as he finished having his jollies and copy the video to his computer. David was much kinkier than I'd ever imagined he would be.

I soon discovered the logic of the number system that the camera used, so I was able to figure out which was the latest without having to watch every one. Even though there were only five, I didn't want to watch any more than I had to. It was bad enough I had to watch this at all.

I looked at the fourth one and there was David with someone that looked kind of familiar, but his back was turned to me. It could have been Harold, but I wasn't sure. The quality on the camera wasn't great so some of the shots were good while others were terrible. On this particular video, nothing much happened. If David was trying to get some action that day, I'm sure he was disappointed because the guy left and then David walked towards the cam and turned it off. I was hesitant to look at the last video. What if I saw something that was ghastly, like David actually committing suicide. Well, I guess it would finally give me closure and I didn't have to investigate anymore.

Let's face it, every time I found out something else about David, it was like David was a very complicated person and did a lot of things I certainly wasn't doing. At some point, I knew enough, I didn't want to know anymore. There is such as thing as too much information and right now I probably knew more about David's private life than anyone else, except those that were participating in private with him.

So I finally pulled the trigger. The first shot was David walking away from the camera naked, seemingly alone. He went to his bed. Then when I saw the next person come in naked I almost fell off my chair. I couldn't believe it. All this time he had been trying to be so helpful to me and trying to do things for David and all along he knew what happened. I couldn't believe it. I tried to calm myself down and said, it's ok Mandy, maybe this is nothing, maybe this was going on and he never recorded the day he died. Maybe this happened on a different day. But still I was flabbergasted, because I was obviously lied to.

I continued to watch and then, what seemed like an innocent gesture, turned into something I will never forget. He gave David a glass of water. David drank it, sitting on the bed. While David drank, he just stood there. After about two minutes David started to choke and held his throat like he couldn't breathe. The other person stood and watched doing nothing.. David was in a panic because he couldn't breathe. David reached out to him for help. He did nothing. He just stood there. It seemed like David was definitely changing colors.

At one point David collapsed on the bed, with one arm hanging off the side. The man watched for five minutes while David laid there. At one point, he lifted David's arm and let it drop to see how far gone David was. David's arm dropped like a stone again over the bed.

Then the man went off-screen. into the next room. When he came back, he was fully dressed. He took one of the sheets, and wiped the glass down. Then holding the glass with the sheet on the rim, he took David's hand and wrapped it around the glass. He put the glass with the remaining fluid by the bedside,. He looked over David one more time. And then he left. The tape continued to play for another couple of hours. The footage of David lying dead in his own bed went on and on. It probably continued to record until the batteries on the nanny-cam died.

I had broken out in a cold sweat; my hands were freezing. I was white as a sheet. I wanted to throw up, I was so sickened by what I just saw. I saw a trusted human being murder another. Somebody that I had believed in had cold bloodedly murdered another person. Meanwhile, they were together and having relations. All this time, he was trying to be cooperative and helpful to me. All along, he was the one that had killed David. I had the proof. I said to myself, I should go and bring this to the police. I should call Fred right now and tell him that David had been murdered.

But then what happened if the police didn't accept this as proof? You read all the time of people who are caught on a camera red handed doing something but because they were recorded without their knowledge, they couldn't use that evidence. Seriously. Somebody murders somebody else and it's clear as day on a video and you can't convict them because their rights were violated?? I just didn't know. But if I brought the police in now, they might just bring him in for questioning and let him go cause of whatever. Some technicality.

This was a soundless video. But you could clearly see it was him. A smart lawyer could turn this around and say that David was sleeping that there's no proof that this was a murder. The dates were screwed up so you couldn't tell when it was recorded. And they would say I had tampered with the evidence and that was another way to throw this out of court. Basically, with the right lawyer, you can get away with murder. It happens every day. And here it was happening in front of me, with people I knew. People I trusted. I was truly losing my faith in humanity.

Still I had to find a way to expose this guy in public where there would be an outcry. There would just be too many people seeing the same thing I saw, that could act as witnesses, that could clearly see that this all added up to the same thing. No, I had to expose him at David's memorial. I know he was going to be there, he would show up. That way I could expose him publicly and when found out publicly, he may react differently and further hang himself. It was a chance I had to take.

And yes, I may get in trouble doing this. Fred would be furious with me. But you know what, I had to avenge David's death. I mean, over the last couple of days I discovered a David I never knew, but a person that had obviously lost his way in life. Nothing he did deserved death, and with some guidance, he could have straightened out his life. But nobody deserved to be murdered for this. I don't know what the motive was, but it could have been something really stupid. Usually, it is.

The show was the day after tomorrow. I had to figure out a way to replace my current Powerpoint presentation with this footage and then expose the killer while he's standing there in public. I think the shock would be enough to push him over the edge. I didn't trust anybody to be a conspirator. Well, maybe Jill. But I really needed Katie to change the video without asking questions. I didn't want to tip off anybody that I was going to expose David's murderer. It would not go over so well at an art show. Not the done thing.

Luckily this was a low resolution video so it didn't take as much memory as a high resolution video. I could easily put it into a PowerPoint. The next question is, how to change the file I already gave Katie? I could ask Katie not to look at the file, that this was highly important. But she would look at it anyway and she might blow the whole thing. I needed help with this plan.

Jill I could trust. I knew I could tell her this and she would keep her mouth shut. She would disagree with me on what I'm doing but she would keep her mouth shut. While I still had the courage, I inserted the video into a PowerPoint, named it the same as the file I had originally given. Now, I just had to figure out how to get this past Katie, so that she would just think it was the same file as before. It was going to be a bigger file, I was just hoping that she wouldn't notice it was bigger.

The next day I was walking around in a fog. People would talk to me and I had a delayed reaction. People asked me if I was ok, I said yeah, just not feeling well. I was truly not feeling well, but mostly mentally. I was still in shock as to what I had seen. I kept looking at Katie to see when she would leave her desk, but each time, it wasn't for long. Certainly not long enough for me to put a flash drive in and copy a file. This was going to be harder than I thought. And there was no guarantee that she wasn't going to look at it, even if I did manage to copy it to the machine if she was gone to the bathroom.

At one point I walking to the copier and somebody rounded the corner sharply and I screamed, I had been so freaked out that somebody came out of nowhere. I tried to laugh it off that I wasn't expecting them, and they accepted it, but the truth was, I was completely nervous and afraid. I was no good at this sort of thing. I was never a good liar and this would be the most underhanded thing I ever did in my life, go to someone's computer and replace the file I had given them earlier, with one that showed somebody being murdered.

The day grew later and later and soon everybody would go home and I would have missed my chance. I kept debating whether I should trust Katie, but she was younger and I don't know how she was going to react, if she was going to show her friends, if she was going to be so freaked out she was going to mess it all up tomorrow. As the end of the day drew near, I was completely on edge. I wanted to get to Katie's computer, but was too scared. I didn't know what to do. Eventually the day ended and we went home. I felt like such a failure that I had wasted an opportunity to get this video so that it could be seen the next day. I had blown it.

I went home. I was angry with myself, angry with everyone. Roger must have sensed that something was wrong and he rubbed himself against my legs. That brought me back to earth and reminded me that there were other things. I still had time, I still had the video. I would find a way to do this. I would have to call Jill and get her to help with this. She was much better at planning devious things and I obviously could not do this alone. I needed support, I needed a trustworthy accomplice. Obviously, today had been a washout. But once I ran this by Jill, I'm certain that she would come up with something. Maybe with her around even I would come up with something. Two heads are better than one they say. We'll see.

With trembling fingers, I dialed Jill's number. She picked up right away, probably thinking I was asking her out for coffee or something.

"Hi Jill, I know that this is going to sound completely off the wall, but I have found definitive proof that David was murdered. I need your help to expose the killer."

"What? Mandy, are you sure about this?"

"Yes, completely, absolutely sure. Can you come over and help me figure this out."

"Are you kidding? I'll be right there"

Jill arrived at my place within 10 minutes.

"Ok, what happened? Have you been drinking? Cause you have got to be one hundred percent sure about this, or I'm going to think you've lost your marbles."

"Listen, while helping Margot the other day, I found this video. I'm going to let you watch and let you be the judge."

Jill watched the video, her eyes got wider and wider.

"I can't believe that guy, he has been so helpful and made us feel so trusting. All the while he killed David. I just can't believe it. And it was so calculated. He just poisoned him and walked away."

"I know, I know, every time I see it, I get sick to my stomach. Jill, how am I going to show this at tomorrow's show?"

"Wait, you're not going to show Fred this?"

"Jill there are all these technicalities about videos being used as evidence and with the right lawyer, this guy could walk. There would be no justice. I have to expose him in public. He's going to be there tomorrow and it's the only chance I'm going to get to avenge David's death. I sensed from the start that this wasn't a suicide. And this proves it. If I show it to Fred, they're going to go through the due process of the law and for all we know this guy could skip town and become a fugitive. I gotta expose him in public, in front of all those witnesses and all those people that know him as well. There's no way he's going to get away with it."

I could see that I was getting to Jill and that she was seeing why this wasn't an easy thing to do.

"Did you talk to Katie?"

"I didn't know if I could trust her. I mean, maybe she would cooperate, but you gotta admit, this is a terrible situation. Some people don't want to be involved with stuff like this and I don't blame her. She's just a young woman. This could give her trauma. I wanted to do it behind her back, but how? She's going to be working the laptop tomorrow at the show and it's already 9PM. How am I going to get this in her computer without her knowing?"

I could see that the wheels inside Jill's head were turning.

"Don't you open the store 3 days a week??"

"Yes."

"Well?" She looked at me with her head cocked.

"Well what?"

"We could go in tonight, while nobody is there and you could load the file on her computer".

A smile crept up on me. I was so engulfed in so many complicated scenarios that I had forgotten I had a key to the gallery. Jill was right.

"Hey, that would work!"

I was the girl Friday of the office. I did everything. I kept everyone's passwords, because everyone kept losing them. I could easily get into Katie's computer.

"Ok, but if were' going to do it it's gotta be now, cause otherwise I'm going to lose my nerve. And you gotta come with me, for support or I'll chicken out."

Jill said, "Bring Roger."

"What?, Bring Roger? That would be something else to make this more difficult."

"Look, this is the plan. We're going to go into your office when it should be closed right?"

"Right."

"Well, if anybody catches us in there, you're going to say that you forgot something you bought for the cat. You have the cat with you, and I'm with you, so it's just going to look like Mandy and her cat and Jill at the mall. Two women and a cat are going to be perfectly respectable. Nobody is going to suspect we're up to no good. You just went there to get something you forgot."

"Of course, that would definitely work!"

I would have never come up with something like that. I would have been too nervous and afraid that I would be caught.

"Ok, let's go!"

CHAPTER ELEVEN

We got to the office at about 9:30PM and some nearby businesses were still open. The office was on the second floor, where all the businesses were closed. I got my keys out and made sure to shut off the alarm. I didn't want any alarms going off bringing the cops sooner. Even though we still had an alibi, I wouldn't get a chance to upload the video. The door opened up easily and I didn't put on the lights on purpose because I wanted to do this as quickly as possible, get in and get out. There were lights on in the hallway. Jill stood inside the store by the door holding Roger by his collar.

I turned on Katie's computer and went to my desk to get the password for her machine. By the time I got back, the machine had booted up and I typed in her name, then the password and I was in. I pulled out the thumb drive where I had the file I was going to swap. I did a search for my name and found the directory where my file was, I then copied the new file over to the same directory. Since there was already a file there by the same name, the computer asked me "the file that you're trying to copy already exists, would you like to overwrite it?". I said yes, and it started to copy the file. My nerves made the process feel longer.

Then my heart jumped into my throat.

I heard a voice that said, "Hello, what are you doing here?" It was Charles, the security guy. He had caught us. Meanwhile the file was still copying. I heard Jill start talking to him, "Oh hi Charles, long time no see."

Charles liked Jill and he was always trying to get the courage to ask her out. In my head I kept saying *go on Jill, keep talking.* I was also talking to the computer in my head saying, *hurry up, hurry up!* I kept asking myself, why is this file transfer so slow? This is crazy, this doesn't happen during the day. Finally the file copied and I shut off the computer the moment it was finished.

Jill said to Charles, "Fancy meeting you here."

He said "I might say the same about you, it's after hours you know."

I walked out of the back and said, "Oh hi Charles" with a smile. I hoped it wasn't obvious how nervous I was.

Jill asked him, "Charles did you get an earring?" Charles was always self conscious around Jill.

"Well yes, I got it last week, do you like it?"

"I think it looks great. Did you get it here in the mall?"

"Yeah, I just got it on a whim"

"Well, you should got it a long time before. It gives you what the French call Diablerie"

"Really?"

"Yeap"

I could see that Charles was getting uncomfortable. So, after a couple of seconds, he changed the subject.

"So, what are you two doing here?"

"Well Charles," I said, "it's just that I had bought

something for my new cat Roger," I pointed down to Roger who was just sitting on the carpet cool as could be, "and I left it behind. Jill and I were in the neighborhood and decided to pick it up.

"Well, I saw some lights and activity coming from here and the door open and I thought I would investigate. Just between you and me, we had a robbery here recently in one of the other offices, and we have to be on the lookout for unusual activity."

"Oh no, we were just leaving, as a matter of fact, I found Roger's toy."

We moved toward the door while Jill continued her conversation with Charles.

"So Charles, I'm going to be around the mall tomorrow to get some lunch. I'll check to see if you're free, maybe you can join me?"

"Yeah, sure," Charles said.

Jill had been a lifesaver. I would have totally lost it.

We left the mall and got in the car. Jill asked, "Did you upload the file?"

"Yes, but it took forever, I didn't know what was happening. I keep hoping that Katie won't see that this file is much bigger and won't pay too much attention to it. To tell the truth, she really doesn't care about the memorial, she's only helping because she knows that this means a lot to me. I think if it had been anybody else, she probably wouldn't go. So I lucked out on that."

We went to Joanie's for a night cap.

"Jill, let's talk about something else cause I'm so nervous that if we start to talk about this, I think I'm going to faint."

"I know what you mean, I was pretty shaken up too by what I saw, so yeah, I'm not too keen on any repeats. Tomorrow will be another day and you can plan how you're going to do this at the show."

We sat at Joanie's having coffee and pastries and Joanie brought a saucer of milk for Roger. It was great to see him drink like he hadn't had milk in weeks.

"You know, after talking to Charles, I definitely think I'm going to ask him for lunch tomorrow."

"Oh?"

"Yeah, I know he likes me, but he's shy and he's actually a nice guy. I haven't been on a date for a while now, so maybe, socialize with Charles a little and see how that goes."

"I didn't know you liked him."

"I don't dislike him, it's just that I haven't had anybody for a while now, and in the past, I thought that he was too straight, but now I realize, he's just shy and probably just lives in his own head most of the time. Plus, it's been a couple of years now, so maybe we have both changed to the point where we can make a go of this."

"Well, I'm glad that tonight's escapade opened up a romantic opportunity for you."

"It's just one of those things. You don't think about somebody and then he just shows up out of nowhere and you start seeing him in a different light. It's like an opportunity that comes out of nowhere."

"Well, I'm just glad that at least part one of this operation is over."

"You know I'm going take a video of this, don't you?"

"Yes, I figured with your social media infatuation and the cataloguing of your daily life, somehow, someway you were going to catalog this event."

"Well, it's not just a social media event. This will act as all the substantive evidence you need to press charges against this guy, and this video will be a complete record of everything that happens that evening."

"That's true the video will be the proof. If it turns into one of these he said, she said, the video will also be proof of what was done."

"Great, so at least we have a plan. I won't put it online right away, and I'll definitely edit the gory parts. But eventually it will appear online."

"Unless Fred objects to putting the video online."

"Fred may not know about it till its' too late" Jill said, smiling.

"I hope he doesn't get angry, or worse yet, it turns the tables in favor of our killer"

"Nah, I'll be careful. If Fred says we can't upload the video, I'll work with him. I want this guy caught too, you know."

Joanie came back to pick up Roger's milk bowl and to play with Roger.

Joanie said, "You know Mandy, you've had Roger for less about a week and he seems so attached to you. He sits and plays as though he's been doing this for years with you. A very relaxed cat."

"Yes, you should see him at home when he plays with his toys. He really didn't take long to adapt to his new living quarters. I think with his old owner, he was just lonely and wanted attention. With me, of course, he gets all the attention he could ever want and more. Actually, while she's here, we have to thank Jill here, cause this was her plan all along. She has been trying for the longest time now for me to get a new cat. And her plan finally worked. So, I'm grateful to her that it turned out to be Roger."

"I even let her in early so she could have her pick of cats without competition from others."

"Well, however he came to you, he is one great cat" Joanie said. "He's always welcome here. You know I love cats as much as you do."

"Well, I'll think that Roger is going to have a lot of admirer's at Joanie's."

We all laughed. Roger looked at us with an expression as if to say: "What?, What's so funny?"

After getting home, I sat on the sofa with Roger on my lap. His contented purrs calmed me. I thought about the events of tomorrow and I grew nervous, questioning if I would be able to pull this off. People would be coming to see an art show. I was going to expose a murderer. Well, I'd gone this far, I was just going to have to finish it. I've uncovered so much this week, that the David I knew seemed like a stranger. But he still was my friend.

I had to view what I was about to do as an exercise. I had to detach myself emotionally. Otherwise, I wouldn't be able to do it. At least, not well. A big part of me wanted to go to the police and tell Fred everything. Let the police handle it.

But I couldn't risk getting into legal trouble- though I knew it was a possibility anyway. I didn't care much at that point. As long as the criminal who killed David wouldn't walk freely.

The more I thought about it, if David had lived, I'm sure he would have eventually made amends on the business end. He would have found another company to outsource the painting of the portraits, or even to do the portraits himself and eventually delivered the pictures for those people. I just felt I knew David well enough that although he may disappoint, he eventually would make good on his promises.

Maybe he would have gotten out of this phase where he had become a pothead. It just seemed that he was sabotaging and self destructing his life. Except that it didn't end because of him, it was somebody else's decision that ended his life for him.

I had calmed down enough that I decided to give the Tarot cards one more try and see what they showed as possibilities for tomorrow. I did it a couple of times, and each time, it showed negativity, it showed violence. Great, that's just what I didn't need. Maybe the cards were wrong. I told myself that about Roger, but the cards had been right about Roger. I'd have to brace myself for the possibility of everything and anything going wrong.

I calmed myself down a little bit by telling myself that I wouldn't be alone. It wouldn't be the murderer and me alone in a room. It would be a room full of people, and once the video was shown, and the people saw what it was, if he tried anything, somebody would stop him, if not out of a desire to protect me, then it would be out of outrage at what they had seen. And Jill said that she was going to film the whole thing. So, there would be plenty of evidence.

I went to bed and I finally fell asleep at around six in the morning. All night long I kept imagining what might happen tomorrow. I got up shortly after that to get to work. Not a good way to start the day.

CHAPTER TWELVE

Thankfully, the day involved a lot of moving around the gallery, cleaning things up, making sure that tables were set up for hors d'oeuvres and wine, looking at the guest list, setting up the area where both Bernard and myself were going to talk. It was a makeshift stage with a screen behind us for the images from the projector.

Bernard would be the first to speak and introduce the gallery, the exhibit and the significance of it all. My original presentation was going to be short and sweet and that would have been the end of it. In light of recent developments, there would be nothing sweet about my new presentation.

I had a big checklist of things to do in the gallery and was checking off the things that had been done and what we had yet to get done for the exhibit. Most of the people we invited were going to come, as well as David's friends and acquaintances that I had gathered for the funeral. And Harold. He was going to be there.

It was a good thing I kept busy. Running around completing tasks didn't exactly leave time for me to panic.

I met Jill on my coffee break and she explained how she had prepared her phone that day's filming. One way or another she believed that the film would constitute complete evidence when the hammer came down. Charles came to our table, to talk to Jill under the pretense of saying hi.

Jill said "Charles, are you going to be around later? Maybe we could get lunch?"

He was acted like he was taken aback but he finally said "Sure".

At some point I was going to be able to go home, change and feed Roger. But for now, I seemed to be falling down this vortex in which every hour brought me closer to doing one of the strangest things I've ever done in my entire life.

I went back to the office, and again was caught up in the whirlwind of putting the show together. There is a lot of preparation that goes into an art show.

Finally, I managed to go home, take a shower and try to do another reading with the cards. I wanted to see if I anything had changed. Like the night before, the cards did not point to a favorable outcome. They said there was danger ahead. Now this could also just have been my whole state of mind. I was not exactly the most cool, calm and collected.

The time came to go to back to the gallery. I took Roger with me to make it look like everything was normal. Jill would look after him while I was doing my thing. Besides he was usually very good in public spaces. This should be no different. Apparently, everybody we invited had decided to attend. Everybody was there. The light of the projector was on the screen, ready for the presentation. I saw Katie fidgeting in the back.

I had to warn her, I had to at least give her a chance to get away. I owed her at least that much. No telling how she might react if she saw this.

I pulled her aside and said, "Can I talk to you? Listen,

last night I changed the presentation I'm going to give now. I can't tell you what it's about, but when it comes time for me to do my presentation, after you press the play button when I say go, just walk away. Things are going to get very ugly and there's no reason that you need to stick around. I'm just warning you so it doesn't come as a surprise."

"You found something?"

"Katie, I found something humongous and things are going to get very crazy when it comes out tonight."

I felt much better getting that off my chest. I hated lying to people or dragging them into something that they were not responsible for. She didn't seem fazed by the news, but at least I felt I had done the right thing. People continued to pour into the gallery Margot was there, Harold was there. Everybody that needed to be there was there so that when I unmasked the killer, he would be in the audience where he couldn't escape.

The moment I had dreaded so much had come. Bernard got up to do his presentation.

"Thank you all for coming tonight. As always, it gives me great pleasure to do another show of outstanding paintings by one of our local artists. However it is with great sadness that I make this presentation this evening. Our present artist, David Towsky, has recently passed away. Nevertheless, his art is here and that is what we're celebrating tonight, the artwork of a talented artist whose vision will inspire all those that experience his work."

There was light clapping and Bernard went on.

"I originally met David thanks to the efforts of one my talented employees, Mandy Cummings, who is standing over there."

As he pointed at me I did a half-hearted wave and as much of a smile as I could muster and there was light clapping in the room.

"And after seeing David's paintings, I knew they would be an invaluable asset to the gallery and to our mutual benefit. So, I hope that you enjoy them and that some of you may be inspired enough to take one of them home with you tonight. You are all welcome to visit the gallery at any time, since we have regular shows of local artists and artists that deserve more recognition both locally and globally. I truly hope this place can become a hub and meeting place for the artistic community. Again, thank you for coming. I think Mandy has some words she would like to say shortly."

There was clapping all around and towards the end there was a picture of David on the screen and people clapped at that as well. Bernard stepped away to talk to different people.

Then came my turn to speak. *Pull yourself together*, I told myself. *This will be over before you know it.*

"Ladies and Gentlemen, thank you for coming tonight for David's art show. I have known David since my college days and I really wanted to give a brief presentation of David's past as an artist. Unfortunately, that's is not what I'm doing tonight."

Big "ooohhh" around the audience.

"It has been said that David Towsky committed suicide. Unfortunately, that is not the truth."

More "oooooohs" and "what?" From the audience

"The truth is that he was murdered. And the murderer is Bernard Jacovski, David's secret lover, Katie play the presentation."

"What's" and all kinds of murmurs filled the room. Bernard was in the other room mingling. He must not have heard because he did nothing to stop me.

I pointed at the screen where parts of David's video

was displayed in full view of everyone.

"In this video, as you can see, that is a naked David in his bedroom walking away from the camera. Now thirty seconds later, who should walk into his bedroom but Bernard, naked and bringing David some water."

People were talking, shushing, saying "wow", and there was all kind of murmuring. A lot of people were taking out their cell phones and were taping my presentation.. I looked at Jill and she just gave me a thumbs-up. Margot stood like she was made of stone. I continued.

"You can see David drinking and Bernard standing there."

Bernard had walked back into the room and started to scream, "stop this video!, stop this right now!" He was heading for me, but Harold and others held him.

"Now, unbeknownst to most, David had an allergy to opioid pain killers. Notice how David is choking and Bernard is not offering any help. He is standing there passively while David is clearly reaching out to him for help. David continues to choke and is now gasping for air. Eventually as you can see, David collapses onto the bed."

"Stop this video right now, I demand this video be stopped!" Bernard was still trying to lunge at me but Harold and some others held him back. Harold told Bernard to shut up and allow me to finish. Katie was still by the laptop and she gave him the one finger salute. The anger in Margot's face was immense, and she stood there glaring at Bernard.

I continued.

"Notice how Bernard finally raises David's arm and lets it drop, to make sure that David is completely unconscious. Bernard disappears for a while and now comes back dressed. See how he cleans the glass with a sheet for his prints. Now he takes David's hand and puts it around the glass so that only David's prints appear on the glass. And then he walks away."

At this point, Bernard broke free from Harold and the others that were holding him and he pulled out a gun. He yelled,

"Everybody just stay away!"

Then he ran towards me and I thought this is the end, he's going to shoot me. Instead he grabbed me by the neck with his arm, put the gun to my head and he was screaming

"You had to go around snooping, didn't you, you just couldn't let it rest that your little friend didn't commit suicide. You meddling idiot! You ruined everything!"

"But why Bernard, why did you kill him?"

"Cause he was going to expose me, he was going to tell the world that I was gay!"

I couldn't believe what I had just heard.

"Bernard, people are coming out every day, what made you think that this was going to be something terrible? If anything, you didn't have to hide anymore. You could live in the truth."

Still screaming, with the gun pointed at my head he said, "Because you idiot, in case you haven't noticed, I'm an orthodox Jew and my wife would have divorced me. She's a very religious woman and she's the one with the money. You think I'd marry a fat ugly broad if she wasn't rich? I would have lost everything, I would have had no money."

"Wait, you mean to tell me that you killed David because you didn't want to lose your meal ticket? Bernard, you're despicable! You destroyed a human life so you could continue to enjoy living a life of luxury and all David was trying to do was help you."

"He wasn't helping me out, he wanted to ruin my life!"

"Answer this Bernard, how did you know he was allergic to opioid painkillers?"

"Cause I've been addicted to them for years, ever since my car accident. I was started on them to relieve the pain of broken bones and eventually I couldn't stop using them all the time. I told him this and he told me about his allergy. In the end, I knew exactly how to eliminate David. You see, I'm very clever when I want to be!"

He was sounded crazier and crazier as he spoke. I was afraid at some point he was just going to shoot. He continued

"Anyway, enough talking, I'm getting the hell out of here before the police come and you're going to be my hostage."

All this while, his mike was still on, so he sounded loud and insane.

"If anybody tries to stop me, I'll kill her. She ruined my life, I have a good mind to kill her anyway. But right now, I'm getting out of here."

He had his arm around my neck and he dragged me as he moved away. At one point he pointed his gun to the audience and said, "If anybody tries to play the hero, I'll kill you too!"

But in that split second that he pointed the gun at the audience, a flash of grey fur, teeth and claws jumped at Bernard's arm. Bernard screamed with pain as Roger dug his nails into his arm and bit his hand. He dropped the gun. All that could be heard was angry meowing and biting a clawing with one paw, while he held on with the other paw and two legs. Bernard tried to shake Roger off, but he couldn't, Roger's nails were deep in his arm. At one point, Bernard tried to bring his other arm around to pry Roger off, but he had to let go of me.

I jumped away from Bernard and at that point Roger jumped at Bernard's face and head. He was scratching and biting like only a pissed off cat would. Bernard screamed, "Get this cat off me, get this cat off me!"

Bernard tripped and fell on his back, and there was an audible *thud* as his head hit the ground. Security guards and other people were running to Bernard and in the distance, the sirens of cop cars blared. When the security guards reached Bernard, one of them tried to grab Roger. Roger jumped off Bernard's head and ran. I called out, "Roger baby, come back, come back!" The security guards had cuffed Bernard, and blood streamed from his head, and his arm was pretty cut up too.

While the security guards held him, Margot walked up to Bernard, spit on him, and said, "You disgusting, worthless piece of crap, you killed my son so that you could continue your charade. At least my son was man enough to be himself. You're just a joke and a killer. I hope you rot in hell!"

Harold led Margot away and said "Come on Margot, he's not worth it, let the cops handle him." Fred and his deputies arrived, with their guns out. Charles and the other security guard had Bernard cuffed and Charles said "Here, he's yours. The gun is on the floor we haven't touched it."

An ambulance had also arrived because, as I learned later, there were conflicting reports that a madman was shooting down a whole crowd at the mall. The paramedics cleaned the blood from Bernard thinking at first he was a victim. Then they were told he was the perpetrator, but they still had to clean off the blood.

Amazingly, Jill continued to film to the very end, even the entrance of the police and the ambulance workers. She knew that this was a once in a lifetime event. She probably felt morally bound to record everything to document the crime. I'm also sure she had visions that this was going to be the video of the month on social media, once she published it.

***

Roger continued to run. After that guy tried to grab him, he wasn't taking any chances. Run away. He started to think. *That guy wanted to hurt Mandy, but I got him good. He's not going to hurt anybody, anytime soon, that weasel. Wait a second, what's a weasel?* He continued running till he got to the parking lot.

***

Colin sensed something terrible had happened and appeared by Roger. He could see now, the shock of him saving Mandy was beginning to bring out his cop persona. He had to work fast or things could go downhill from here. He could become a man trapped in a cat's body.

"Roger, look at me."

Roger looked up and he sort of recognized this man.

"Now listen Roger, we're going to play a game. It's called chase the light. Look at this tiny ball of light. Can you catch it? Whoa, it's too fast for you. Go ahead, try again. Nope, too fast for you. Look Roger, it's moving away, chase it Roger, see if you can catch it."

With a small, battery-operated laser pointer, Colin distracted Roger so his cat persona would come back. Roger kept chasing the ball of light and Colin kept luring him away from danger.

***

I continued to look for Roger, he was nowhere to be found. There was a lot of confusion. Cops talking, cop radios, ambulance radios, security guards, people milling about, and Roger was nowhere to be seen. I hoped he didn't get hurt in that whole escapade. I was amazed at how he went berserk because he saw that I was in danger. Maybe this was something he picked up from his previous owner. Maybe she'd lived in a bad neighborhood and he was constantly chasing away bad guys. Who knows?!

The amazing thing was that he knew when the trouble was real He'd only lashed out when he'd sensed that I was in danger. Otherwise, he had been completely calm. Somehow, my cat knew the difference between people with good intention and people with bad intentions. But he was lost now. Or at least not within my line of sight.

By now Jill had gotten all the footage that she needed.

"Well, I have all the proof and a blow by blow account of this guy going nuts so that there's no way he's getting out of it. Not to mention you have the original tape from David. And since his wife will find out all about this, believe me, he's not going to be able to afford any kind of fancy lawyer.

"Hey, you did good kiddo. I could see you were a little nervous at first but then you were determined that the world know about this horrible crime. And you were able to show the whole thing in front of an audience so, there are plenty of witnesses, plenty of people holding him back.

"It was horrible that Margot had to see this but you know what, she'll be able to press charges if the police need anybody to. I mean, I don't know exactly what happens in these types of cases, this is so weird and there are so many angles to this situation that this guy is toast one way or another. Unfortunately in New Jersey they don't have a death penalty. So they won't give him that. But they'll probably give him a 100,000 year sentence. But it might get cut in half for good behavior." And she smirked.

"Thanks Jill, for going the extra mile, for everything. I'm so glad that it's over, and even though I was terrified when he grabbed me and was threatening to shoot me, I thought it was all worth it to have him caught by the police. I just have one problem now. Roger has disappeared."

"Disappeared! Oh, we gotta go look for him. I haven't

spent years trying to find you a cat that would be great for you, for him now to disappear over a teensy weensy thing like disarming a criminal and laying into him with all his might" she said sarcastically. "I have to tell you, Roger was GREAT! I got great footage of him going ballistic on that guy. See, he knew you were in danger, he figured out a way to attack the enemy and he was very sneaky about it. He knew exactly when to pounce. I never believed there was such a thing as an attack cat, but Roger is definitely the closest thing to an attack cat I've ever seen."

We went to look for him. As we were walking out, Fred said, "Mandy, I need a statement from you." I said, "Fred I gotta find my cat, can I give it to you tomorrow?"

Jill cut in, "Fred, I got the whole thing videotaped, from soup to nuts. I'll make you a copy and drop it off at the station so you can watch the whole thing tonight. Believe me, it's a blow by blow account of everything that happened tonight and what this guy did. And it's in high definition, so the details are very clear."

Jill had been doing videos for a long time, so I was sure that her video was news station quality. And she had the most super duper phone camera that could rival any regular camera.

Fred said, "Ok, but Mandy, in my office tomorrow."

"No problem Fred, I'll be there."

So we walked all around the area outside the gallery. They had CSI type people combing the gallery. I don't know what they were looking for, since there was a whole video of the thing. But they didn't know that and that's what they probably do in all these situations. So, they continued doing their job.

We went downstairs to the lower level of the mall. We had to go through a police barricade, they had sealed off the whole top floor. I kept saying to myself, *where could Roger be?* Maybe he was hiding. He was a smart cat, but I was still worried. Maybe he got hurt, maybe Bernard managed to punch him? I really hoped not.

We went out to the parking lot hoping that he would be out there. But it was night time and we couldn't find much of anything, let alone a cat. I would have to put lost cat posters up all over town saying "have you seen this cat?". I really hope I didn't lose Roger entirely. I would be supremely sad if he was lost for good. Where could I find another cat like him? Roger was a special cat. Just in the week that I'd had him, he had shown himself to be very different than the vast majority of cats.

Somewhere in this town was my cat. Hopefully safe, unscathed and away from all the confusion.

Eventually, Jill talked me out of looking for Roger any longer. We had gone around the mall, looking here, looking there, asking people if they had seen a large grey tabby. We did this for at least one and a half hours. No Roger.

We went to Joanie's to get some coffee and blow off steam. These had been some of the tensest hours in all my life. I nearly lost my life in the process. Thanks to my cat I was saved. Again, I started to think of Roger.

Joanie asked "Where's Roger?"

"He's lost"

"Lost? What happened?"

We gave her a recap of the night and how we had spent over an hour and a half looking for him. Joanie said

"Well, he's probably hiding somewhere in the mall area, but in the dark it's going to be awfully hard to find a cat. Try again early tomorrow, by then the drama of the evening may have worn off".

We ordered pastries and Katie walked in a little while later and joined us. She gave me a hug and said I was very brave, that was definitely the heaviest thing she had seen in all her life. She asked where Roger was, I explained to her that he appeared to have gotten lost. But I was hopeful that he would turn up.

Even though it was late, we left Joanie's and went to "The Path to Perdition" a favorite bar of ours that was open until the wee hours. In spite of the name, it was just a homey neighborhood bar, where you could just have a drink and nobody bothered you. They had the local news on in the bar and they were covering the story. We sat and ordered some drinks. It was late, but who cared. It wasn't like I had a job to go to tomorrow. I said to Katie, "Well, it looks like we're out of a job." She laughed.

Katie said, "I never really liked working there and I was just doing it to get something on my resume. I have been looking for a job for a while now and this is just going to hasten my search. I'm pretty confident I would find another job. Somebody needs a graphics artist out there somewhere."

"And here I was hoping to get hired at this place. All the time we were working for a murderer."

After an hour at the bar, we decided to call it a night. We all drove to our respective homes. As I approached mine, a certain emptiness filled me knowing Roger wouldn't be there to greet me. Yes, I had accomplished a lot for the good of a lot of people. But I lost my cat in the process.

I parked my car in the driveway. Locked it and went to the front door. My heart leapt up inside me when I saw the front step. There on the front step of my house was Roger, sitting on his hind legs, attentively looking around. He knew how to come home! I picked him and held him tight and said:

"Oh baby you had me so worried I was looking all over for you. I thought I was going to have to get the marines out for you. You gave me a big scare. But you're my hero.

You saved me from evil. Thank you Roger."

I checked him all over, and nothing, not a scratch. I took my keys out to open the door and told Roger,

"You put up a great fight, are you sure you're not part tiger?"

When I got in, I gave Jill, Katie and Joanie a call to tell them that Roger was waiting for me on the front step of the house. Wasn't that amazing? I had my cat back.

EPILOGUE

The next day I went to the police station to make a statement and speak to Fred. Fred was busy when I first got there, but one of his deputies took my statement. I learned from the deputy that they received the full video of what had happened last night from Jill. He said they've never seen anything like that, where somebody is exposed and then tries to kill somebody else.

He said to stick around that Fred wanted to talk to me. I did and after about twenty minutes, the receptionist said I could go in.

Fred had dark circles under his eyes. This whole thing had kept him up to the wee hours of the morning. I'm sure he got only 2 hours sleep, if any.

"Hi Fred, you look like you've been up all night."

He said, "yeah, for the most part. I'll get right to it Mandy, I'm upset with you with what you did. Why didn't you come to me when you found that tape? You could have died last night if that guy had decided to kill you!"

"Well, I found that tape quite by accident. I really thought of bringing it to you, but here was my through process. Bernard is a wealthy guy. This was a silent tape. I feared that if I just gave it to you, he would get a fancy lawyer and somehow there would be some technicality that because this video was taken without the clients consent that it couldn't be used as evidence in court and that the video doesn't prove anything. It just shows two lovers doing something, but what it is not clear. This kind of stuff happens every day and I didn't want Bernard to get away with this.

"Also, I thought I was safe because I was doing it in a public space, filled with people who would protect me from anything if he got upset. And they did, they restrained him from stopping the video, they were telling him to shut up. But nobody imagined that he was going to have a gun and actually try to kill people."

"That's the thing Mandy, when dealing with criminals, especially these types that are very pre-meditated in their actions, they're usually walking around prepared. If plan A fails, then they go to plan B. I don't think he thought that anything was going to happen at this show. The gun was licensed and he owned it because he thought he might need protection in case of burglars if he worked late nights at the business.

"But I think he walked around with the gun because he was paranoid. And the fact that he would kill David to hide his secret tells you that this guy had serious mental problems. I know you're a good person and you don't think of people with guns and people killing you, but that's the world we live in now. Somebody somewhere is killing someone for no good reason other than they got upset or their hair is curling the wrong way."

"Is there going to be a trial? Am I going to have to be a witness?"

"Well, he's pretty much lost his mind with this experience. He made a formal confession about killing David to protect himself and claimed he acted out of self-preservation last night, he wanted to kill you for exposing him."

"What?"

"That's right, he's lived a double life now for so long, the experience he had last night made him come unhinged. So, there's not going to be a trial. Before the confession, Margot had filed full charges against him and she said she wanted to do whatever it took to get this guy behind bars. Her one regret is that this state doesn't have capital punishment, otherwise, she'd be pushing for that. So, at least she'll get her one wish.

"She's very upset but grateful that the truth came out. We also have Jill's tape. I tell you, she should be a newscaster. She captured that whole video from beginning to end. We have everything on video including his confession that he killed David and that he planned on killing you and anybody else that got in his way. You were right Mandy, David didn't commit suicide. I don't' think Margot ever really believed that either but who would want to kill David? We now know that things were weirder than anybody could have imagined.

"Bernard's wife is in the process of filing for divorce. We brought her in for questioning and had her watch the video. Aside from her shock of what her husband was doing on the side, she didn't appreciate his statement that he married a fat ugly broad only for her money. So Bernard is not going to have any star lawyers representing him. Apparently he has no money of his own, she was the one with the wealth.

"So Mandy, chances are this is a once in a lifetime experience, but if you run into any crimes in the future, please come see me and we'll see what we can do, okay? I want you to live to the end of your days. By the way, that cat of yours is something else. If it wasn't for him, who knows what may have happened. He was the cavalry and the marines all in one."

"Yeah, I'm really lucky to have found Roger. He's very protective of me, but he's also great around people. He lets them play with him and he's just mellow most of the time. He's kind of like Santa Claus, he knows who's naughty or nice."

***

Later that day, I went by Margot's house to check in and see how she was doing. I walked in and the first thing she did was give me a hug. She said;

"Oh Mandy, what a night."

"Listen Margot, I'm sorry I didn't give you a warning about what I was going to show, but, I had to keep this under wraps cause I just wanted this guy to get caught."

"That's okay Mandy. that experience was very cathartic. Thank you for what you did. I know you didn't believe that David had committed suicide any more than I did. It just didn't make sense. As much as I grieve losing him, I'm glad that we now know for sure that he didn't take his own life.

"Before, I just felt that maybe I'd failed him as a mother and he took his life cause of something basic I overlooked. Knowing somebody else killed him doesn't make me jump for joy, but at least, it wasn't anything wrong with him or with me, he was the victim of a crime.

"That took guts Mandy, to stand there in front of all those people and expose this guy. My only regret is that your cat didn't kill him, but at least he weakened him so the cops could get him. But one question that I've had since last night is, where did you get the video?"

"Well Margot, I suspected the teddy bear I took was a nanny cam, a toy with a camera, and I was hoping that would clear up whether David had committed suicide or something else had happened. I needed closure. And sure enough, he didn't, the video proved it. I truly wanted to keep something to remember David by, but I thought that teddy bear would have more treasures."

"I'm glad you're on top of these things, I would have thought it was another of David's stuffed animals. You know, I've walked in that room and I've seen animals there that he had since he was a boy. He was just a gentle artistic boy, he didn't have a mean bone in him. Lapses of judgment from time to time, to be sure, he was a bit of a space cadet. But he never willfully tried to hurt anybody."

"Well, the David I knew was always a gentle soul. Margot, I just want to mention that we may have to deal with some issues regarding David's painting business."

"Oh, what happened?"

I couldn't tell her the entire truth about David having ripped people off.

"Well, apparently, to have time to paint his artsy stuff, David tried to outsource his portrait business. But between the art show and his passing, that kind of went south and he didn't refund the people's money. I think he was in the midst of looking for another outsourcer. In any event there are all these people that gave him deposits and never got a picture. I would be happy to help you in finding out who they were and how much they were owed. We could do this anytime, it's not like they needed this money tomorrow".

"Well, maybe in two weeks, when the dust has settled down from yesterday's events."

"Sure, whenever you're ready Margot, we'll do it."

I went to visit Jill at the animal shelter.

"Hi Jill, how are you holding up from last night?"

"I'm doing alright. I talked to Fred and he told me Bernard made a formal confession, so there's no way he's getting away with this. He told me he loved my tape and that if Bernard hadn't confessed, that would have been all the evidence they needed. Aside from the tape you found.

Oh, and by the way, I'm so glad you're here, I want you to see something you're not going to believe."

She took me to the office to the computer. There was a video on YouTube called "hero cat saves owner from killer". It had over one hundred thousand views.

"I want you to know that this video has been shared on Facebook, tens of thousands of times. Roger is a superstar. Look at all these comments! People just love him."

I read all the comments below the video. People were saying great things about him. She had started the video when Bernard was threatening to kill me or anybody else and Roger jumped on Bernard. The video continued All the way through to when the security guards intervened and the cops arrived. You could hear me in the background yelling "Roger baby, come back". I was amazed that so many people had watched the video, but it just showed how special Roger was. Maybe he thought he was a tiger. But whatever it was, he certainly saved the day.

I got home and Roger was there rubbing himself against my legs when I walked in and I said,

"Roger guess what? You're famous and you're a hero."

I pulled up the video from an email link Jill had sent and showed it to Roger. Plus I wanted to watch it again. "See Roger, that's you in action."

It had been a hectic morning, visiting the police, talking to Margot, and coming down from the complete shock of yesterday's events. It's like I was still full of adrenaline, but at the same time, I felt I had been in a war and had narrowly escaped being shot by the enemy.

I sat and confronted the reality in which I had suddenly found myself. I had no job. Sure, I'd helped a lot of people, and that was great. But there wouldn't be a gallery. Bernard's wife wasn't likely interested in keeping it open.

Bernard himself had probably only kept it open to prove to her that he made money. It also had kept him out of the house and away from his wife. He also enjoyed rubbing elbows with the artists. More than elbows, apparently.

So yeah, I'd gotten justice for David, but had lost a job and all the folks that worked there. Now it was time to see what else I was going to do in the future to earn a living. In the meantime, I was going to have to ramp up my Tarot readings at different restaurants and vanity businesses that could afford to have a Tarot reader as part of the décor.

I would do an astrological chart to see what the planets had to say for the next couple of weeks. Maybe I could find a job writing horoscopes for people. Where would I get such a job? Maybe I'll reach out to some of the local papers.

In the middle of all this, I got a call from Jill.

"Listen, you're not going to believe this"

"What?"

"I got a call from a friend who has connections with an ad agency. Guess what? They saw Roger in the video and they want to use him in a cat food commercial."

"What?"

"Yeah, I have to find out more about it, I don't know if it's a big agency or a small nearby agency. The whole thing about the internet is trends, and right now, Roger is trending. Whatever happens, it's a start. Roger is going to be on tv."

"That's the most incredible thing I've heard. But I have to tell you, after last night, I think anything can happen. I was just sitting around thinking about money, or lack thereof, and what I was going to do for a new job. Do cat food commercials pay a lot? I don't know anything about this?"

"Don't worry, when the time comes I'll help you

negotiate. I know a lot about online marketing and advertising rates and things on the production end of the ads."

"Well, let me know when you talk to them and what is the next step."

I hung up with Jill and I was excited. This could be an amazing prospect if it actually comes to be. This could actually become a job.

"Roger, guess what?? You're going to be in a cat food commercial. You're going to be a tv star!"

Thank you for reading this book

Thank You! If you've enjoyed "Murder at the Art Gallery", would you please take a minute to leave a review on Amazon. Even just a few sentences would be great. When you leave a review it helps others who are looking for new cozy mysteries to read, and it helps me improve the books. Plus I'd love to hear what you think.

Be sure to get your FREE audiobook of "Murder at the Art Gallery here:

http://audiobooksignup.higher-understanding.com.

You'll also be informed of when new books in the series are going to be released.

Thank you, Eleanor Kittering

Murder at the Pet Food Company

NEW BOOK CHAPTER ONE

If today was the tomorrow we worried about yesterday, Mandy's worry had manifested itself again today. Mandy was worried that this tv commercial situation with Roger was not going to come through. She hadn't found any steady work yet and although she was beefing up her tarot readings and looking to see if she did more astrological charts, she was still worrying about her financial tomorrow.

For those that missed the last book, after certain acts of heroism, Roger, Mandy's cat, had become an internet celebrity and there had been offers to appear in a cat food commercial by a local pet food company.

But after a couple of days she hadn't heard anything else about it and nobody had contacted her, so she thought that was just a fluke, somebody thought that was a good idea, but wasn't going to go through with it, and they abandoned the idea at the last minute. So, Mandy was looking around to see how she could better her money situation.

She decided to call up Jill, her best friend, and see if she had any ideas on how to cash in on Roger's new found fame, like other animal people had done on the web. There were plenty of pets out there that were famous just for being cute. There's gotta be a way to get Roger famous for actually saving people from danger. And he was a good looking cat too, so the cute angle could be worked as well. Jill was the internet queen, and if there was a way to get Roger more promotion on the web, Jill would know it.

"Hi Jill, just calling to run a couple of things by you."

"Ok, shoot."

"Well, not having heard anything about this cat commercial, I was just wondering what could I do to cash in on Roger's present fame. I know that some people have blogs of their pets and somehow those become successful. I was wondering if something like that could done with Roger?"

"Sure you can. The first thing we could is set up a blog, where it would be easy to add daily pictures of Roger and allows you to describe certain situations that Roger is going through his daily life. And then you gotta start thinking marketing, maybe T-shirts, maybe mugs. Those are pretty easy. Stuff like a Roger doll is a little harder. But the most important thing is Roger has to have a web presence so the public can easily find him."

"The next thing is to set up a Facebook page, not unlike what we did with David."

Memories of what that turned into sent shivers down Mandy's spine.

"Although the David page became something else entirely, most Facebook pages are actually fun. The David page had way too much drama attached to it, considering the circumstances.

"So, we'll definitely get a Facebook page going that you can send traffic to the blog. That actually is not that hard to do."

Hearing Jill speak made Mandy feel that there were other options that life didn't have to hinge upon whether somebody crawled out of the wood work and made an offer to her. She could create her own opportunities.

"So, how long would this take?"

"Not very long, I could get something started today and we could add and a couple of pictures later, showing that Roger is actually a normal, sweet cat, he was an attack cat because of what happened last time."

For those of you joining in for the first time, the short version of "what happened last time" was, Mandy's boss was threatening to kill her in front of an audience and Roger intervened and took him down. It was the video of this act of heroism that made him a YouTube star, and spurred the cat commercial offers that hadn't materialized yet.

Mandy said "That sounds great, we definitely gotta show the mellow side of Roger, this way people can relate to him as a regular cat."

"Ok, I'll get a couple of things together and we can take it from there."

"Thanks, I'm looking forward to it."

Mandy hung up the phone from Jill and proceeded to find as many cute pictures as she had of Roger. It would give her something to do that made her feel as though this could lead somewhere, that the future would be less grim. Roger sat down next to her and started to purr, always a sign that he was feeling mellow. Mandy showed him pictures on her phone.

"See Roger, that's you over at Joanie's, sprawled out on the floor. And here's you at the park with the leash."

Maybe she could get someone to take a picture of her walking Roger, and that would be the main page picture.

In the middle of all this, phone rang.

"Hello"

"Hello, is this Mandy Cummings?"

"Yes, it is."

"Hi there. My name is Stacy Parks and my company's name is Hedon Pet Nutrition. I was calling you because I am interested in shooting a commercial with your cat Roger as the lead."

Mandy's heart leapt inside her, the commercial was coming through!! "Oh yes, my friend Jill had told me about you, thank you so much for calling Ms. Parks."

"Call me Stacy. And no, the pleasure is all mine. It's not everyday that we get a hero cat to represent Hedon, and I think Roger would be perfect. I've seen that video a couple of times and that was truly an act of selflessness how he attacked that man who was threatening to kill you. He protected you at the risk of his life. Truly a hero cat."

"Well, yes, I feel very lucky to have found Roger and he's been very protective of me from the very start. And the amazing thing is that the rest of the time, he's very mellow and he lets people pet him and play with him all the time. It's only when he senses a situation where I could be harmed that he gets defensive."

"Yes, I think he'll be perfect to represent us. You see, we're a niche cat food brand, we make chicken cat food which is organic but at the same time, we care for our chickens so that we can provide the highest quality cat food possible. We are very unique in the market, and that's why we need a unique mascot and when I saw Roger, I knew we had found our representative."

"I'm so glad, believe me, in person he actually is a very sweet animal, and I think he'll work very well with your product."

"Interesting, I would love to meet him in person. Do

you think you can bring him by tomorrow morning, say about 10AM?"

"Oh sure, that would be great."

"Yes, and we can further speak about the advertising possibilities. I gather he is not representing anyone else right now?"

"No, he's not."

"Good, so we'll start on a clean slate. Also, I would like you to view our company video which is kind of a curriculum vitae which explains the ethos of our company."

"Oh, I would love to see it, please send me the link, here's my email."

Mandy proceeded to give Stacy the email.

"Great. I'll have my assistant send you the link and we'll meet tomorrow. It's been such a pleasure speaking with you."

"Same here Stacy, looking forward to meeting you."

And they hung up. Mandy was super excited and figured with this and the cat blogging project, she might actually be able to make enough money to live and this would become her full time job. She called Jill.

"Hey, guess what?!! I got a call from Stacy Parks from Hedon Pet Nutrition, and she definitely wants to make a commercial with Roger. She was very nice and positive, and she's going to send me a link later to their main company video, which defines their whole company philosophy."

"Hey, that's great. Between that and getting the blog going for Roger, this could become a nice income source for you."

"That's what I'm hoping. I had just about given up on this and then out of the blue, she calls. We haven't talked any money yet, but apparently she's thinking of more than one commercial. What do you think I'll get for this??"

"Chances are for the first one, you'll get some money up front and no residuals. However, if that's successful, then I would negotiate for more money. But take it one step at a time, even if you just get one commercial, you can always go to another company and try to get more work. There are people out there making money with their pets, no reason why you can't try doing the same."

"Yeah, I really hope that this can turn into a regular thing."

"Well, let me try some ideas for the blog, you get some pictures and text for the blog and we'll get together later this week and start putting this together."

"That sounds great, I'm sure excited about all this."

"Me too!"

And with that they hung up. In the midst of that call, Mandy had received an email and she figured that was the email with the link to the company video. She opened it up and sure enough there it was.

The link took her to a very well produced video. It started out with the early morning sunrise and chickens walking out in this country setting, on a well manicured lawn and then, this young beautiful woman picks up one of the chickens and hugs her close and the slow mo shot reveals that she loves this chicken so much. And then, after holding that chicken for a little bit she picks up another chicken.

Then an announcer's voice, in very soft modulated tones starts saying "At Hedon, we really love our chickens. We do everything we can to make them feel especial. There is soft piano music in the background.

The announcer continues "Every day is another opportunity to do our chickens proud and make them feel good. A happy chicken is a thing of joy." More piano music. "We also make sure that our chickens get their rest. Well rested chickens are healthier chickens."

The camera pans to a chicken coop that is paneled in Koa wood and each sitting area for the chickens is covered in a purple satin cushion. "Scientific studies have shown that the right kind of music can have a positive effect on the growth of animals" In the background you can hear them playing Mozart's A Little Night Music, followed by Boccherini's Minuet. There are chickens in the coop which seem to be swaying to the music, as though they're meditating in a semi trance.

The camera switches again and now, the chickens are eating but it's with their own crystal bowl and the corn is piled high on these dishes. They peck at the food elegantly, as though they're quite trained in these matters.

The music continues and the camera changes back to the girl at the beginning, this time she's holding a chicken and smiling at the camera angelically. "At Hedon, we make sure that our chickens are treated to the highest standards. Hedon. It's not just a dream. It's a way of life." As the camera moves back, you see the girl waving goodbye and you see the farm looking very fantasy like with rich saturated colors. And the video fades out.

Mandy was pretty amazed. They really treat their chickens amazingly well. And they're a pet food company. This all must be very organic. Mandy sent Jill the video and called her.

"Jill, you gotta watch the video I got from Hedon Pet Nutrition."

Jill, starts watching and says "Wow, these guys must be a big operation. Or at least a fancy one. Definitely a very unique way of making pet food. I'm sure they're going to do right by Roger"

"That's what I was thinking, I mean, they're very in

tune with the needs of animals."

"Well, you can't go wrong with that, and they seem to have money, so I think you'll make some decent up front money."

"Yeah, that's what I thought too. People who go to these lengths to take care of their farm animals, you figure they gotta take care of the people that work with them."

"Yeah, it's this whole holistic approach to the work force they have nowadays. It's no longer about employees, but that everybody is part of the family and everybody makes a contribution for the future that will benefit everybody. Bringing Roger in will allow their brand to flourish, so Roger and you, of course, contribute to the over business. When are you going to see her?"

"Tomorrow morning. She didn't seem like she was in a rush, so maybe they're just feeling out Roger see how he is in real life and go from there. I told her that he's very mellow in his regular life, it's just when I'm threatened that he gets upset."

"Yeah, once they see how he is in real life, they'll see that he'll become a credit to their brand. And once you have the Facebook page and the blog, you can direct traffic to your Facebook page, with the commercial on the page, and from there hopefully sell some merchandise."

"That would be great. I would so love doing something I like as opposed to another job that I may not be 100% into and this would be something that I could get into for years and years."

"Well, let's hope that this all works out."

She hung up with Jill and now was more than super excited at the prospects lying ahead.

"Roger you're going to be all over the web. You're going to become a regular online superstar."

Sometime later, she gets another call on the phone. At

first thinks it's Jill but it's a number she's not familiar with.

"Hello."

"Hi, is this Mandy Cummings?"

"Yes, this is me."

"Hi, my name is Loretta Gumble and I'm the owner of Fantastic Pets, a pet food and pet toys company."

"Oh, hi there. You know, today must be my day to get calls from pet companies."

"Have you spoken to others?"

"Yes, earlier I was speaking with Hedon foods for the possibility of a commercial."

"I see. Well, I was also going to try to pitch to you that you might consider doing some work with us, but if you're already committed to Hedon, maybe we can talk later."

"Well, nothing is still in stone, so I would be happy to hear what your offer is."

"Ok. We're a small pet company and we make commercials now and then for streaming tv and on the web. We're not as esoteric as Hedon, we just sell pet treats and toys, and thought that Roger would be good for some of our toys."

"Do you know Stacy Parks?"

"Oh yes, we've crossed paths in the past. Let's just say that Stacy has a vision about her products, which is very elegant. Me, I'm happy just to fill certain needs of customers with our toys and treats."

"Have you been doing this long?"

"We've been around for a couple of years. I've always been a pet lover and was always wondering how to make a living working with animals. When the internet came along, I started exploring what was it that people wanted for their pets and started to figure out how to fill those needs. And that's how Fantastic Pets was born."

"Well, that sounds nice. I didn't know you could actually make a living with animals, and now Roger may find a way to do that for me, we'll see if his fame online can generate enough interest."

"Yes, Roger is quite a cat from what I've seen. I'd love to get the opportunity to work with him in the future."

"Well, why don't we do this. Let me speak with Hedon and see what they have to say and how far it goes, since they called me first. Depending on how all that goes, that's not to say that somewhere down the pike, we couldn't do business as well. It really all depends on how it goes with Hedon."

"Ok, that sounds like a plan. I really was mostly calling to introduce myself and tell you a little bit about our business. Call me if the deal with Hedon is not what you thought it was or ends sooner than later."

"I think that's reasonable. Listen Loretta, thanks for calling, I truly appreciate all attention that Roger gets."

"You're welcomed Mandy, here's to working together in the future."

And so they left it at that. Very interesting. This morning I didn't know if I was going to get any commercial work and now I have two offers. Loretta was very nice, not pushy, just asked and left it as a we'll see. I can tell she's an animal lover as well. Well, I have to keep my options open. Maybe not everything works out with Hedon. Or maybe they just want to do one commercial. Whatever happens, I know I'll have one more commercial later on in the future. And it sounds like I'll be working with nice people.

By now, all this thinking about the future was making her crazy. She thought maybe she'd get something to eat over at Joanie's and just relax. That's probably the best. She'd done enough for thinking about the future, for now.

"Come on Roger, we're going to Joanie's!!"

NEW BOOK CHAPTER TWO

The next day was one of those beautiful days where everything is going right. The skies were blue and clear, the weather was nice, a perfect day for anything. Mandy was excited that today might be the day where she gets the first commercial for Roger. She dressed up business casual, dressy but not crazy dressy. Roger was rubbing himself around her feet, hoping to get fed.

"C'mon Roger, it's breakfast time!"

And she laid out one of Roger's favorite foods which he proceeded to eat like it was going to disappear from the bowl.

She thought about the conversations she'd had yesterday about cat commercials. First there was Stacy Parks and her super fancy video. Obviously, that is the job to get, because apparently Hedon Pet Nutrition was a niche brand, but a respected brand in the industry. But she was also glad that she got a call from Loretta Gumble. It didn't make her feel as though this was such a one off thing. Maybe this whole cat commercial thing is bigger than she thought, she just wasn't aware of what was out there. There may be non-pet food commercials, where they just need a cat. This was something she would have to explore.

She was looking at the time and thought, well, it's time to meet Stacy Parks, and put the collar on Roger. She went to the car a little nervous, but excited about this new prospect. Once in the car, she headed off in the direction of Hedon Pet Nutrition. When she got there, she realized she'd passed this building many times while driving down this road. She pulled in the parking lot, parked the car, and let Roger out. She locked the car, and took the leash and went walking over to the building. Inside there were 2 guards that let people into the building, she said she was going to Hedon and they just let her go upstairs. She took the elevator to the 3rd floor and there was a large glass office, which was Hedon's.

It was a very fancy, modern office, a full glass wall that showed a very well designed corporate space, elegant and at the same time modern. There were a lot of offices that had moved to Jersey from New York City over the years, and because the rents were lower, they could dress up their corporate spaces better.

As she walked into the reception area, the secretary asked her who she was there to see. Mandy said she had an appointment with Stacy Parks. She looked at the calendar and said, yes, Ms. Parks is waiting for you please go right in. Mandy walked into an elegant office/personal space. Although the reception area had see through walls, this office had regular walls, to give privacy to the tenants. The poor receptionist was exposed out in the main reception area, for everybody to see as people walked by. However, there weren't many people, that's for sure.

The elegant room seemed to be empty, which gave Mandy a chance to explore the room. She was looking at different awards that Hedon had won in the past, there were corporate pictures of Stacy Parks and several other people, no doubt part of her staff. There was a couple picture of her with a man, no doubt her husband. The whole place gave off this aura of success and glamour. Definitely Stacy Parks was one of those people that when people asked her what her dreams were, she would say, she's just dreaming bigger.

Roger was sniffing around as well, and he leaned again a delicate table that had a long thin vase on top. Mandy said "Roger honey, don't". But that was enough to send the vase falling. It was a long, thin necked vase with a bulbous base, looking very expensive and Mandy was wondering when it broke, how much it was going to cost to replace it.

As it got closer to the ground, Mandy expected a crash but because of the thick carpets, it just landed with a soft thud and rolled to the other side of the room. Mandy heaved a sigh of relief and then ran after it, figuring she'd pick it up and put it back before Stacy Parks showed up. Where was she anyway?? Maybe she had to go to the bathroom. As she got to the other end of the room where the vase had rolled to and bent down to pick up the vase, she noticed a couple of feet sticking out behind a long bookcase. It was Stacy Parks. She was looking quite dead.

For a moment, Mandy was stupefied. She just stood there, holding the vase from the top on one hand and looking down at the body. At that moment, the secretary walks in and asks "What are you doing?" She sees Mandy holding the vase in an upraised arm, and looks down and sees the feet of Stacy Parks and she asks "What did you do, did you hit Ms. Parks!!?? Is she alright?? I'm calling security" Mandy was saying "Wait, I didn't do anything, I just found her!!", but the woman had run out of the room in a panic.

Mandy thought the first thing to do was to put the vase back on its table. She was petting Roger and saying to herself, I got to get out of here, wait no, I gotta call Fred before this gets crazy. I mean, maybe she just fainted, who knows? This is not something I needed. I just came here to do a commercial with Roger and this woman faints on me. Or worse yet, dies. Did somebody kill her? Who would kill Stacy Parks?? In the middle of this, two security guards show up. The secretary yells out, "There she is, I think she attacked Ms. Parks!!" Mandy said "I didn't do anything, I just found her there, I had an appointment with her!" The secretary asked "Yeah, then why were you holding that vase in your hand??"

"My cat knocked it over, we're here to set up a commercial with him. Listen I hope you called a doctor or an ambulance because I don't know if she fainted or something else has happened to her, but she needs medical help now."

"Oh, I called the police they're on their way right now. I've never seen you before and all of a sudden something bad has happened to Ms. Parks. I say that's very fishy, and with that vase, you probably got into an argument with her and then hit her over the head when you wouldn't get your way."

"What??!! I did no such thing. I came into the room and I couldn't find her and I found her lying there on the floor, I had nothing to do with this, it's as much of a surprise to me as it is to you."

The guards were saying, "Miss we're going to have to cuff you until the police get here."

Mandy said "Cuff me?? I didn't do anything!!!"

But as they got closer Roger was making a low guttural sound warning the two security guards. Mandy was saying Roger keep calm, don't get excited. She was holding him by the leash. The guards kept walking towards Mandy and Roger was hissing.

Mandy said "If you get any closer, he thinks you're

threatening me and he will attack. He's already taken down two other men."

One of the guards says, "Wait, I've seen this cat on YouTube, I'm not messing with him."

The other guard says, "I'm not scared of a cat", and lunged at him. Roger jumped on his arm with such force that he knocked him over and scratched up his whole arm. Mandy was saying Roger that's enough.

"I told you not to get closer once he goes berserk I can't control him."

The guard was going to go for a round two when the police finally showed up. It was Fred and Jimmy.

"Police, what's going on here??" "Mandy?" said Fred "Can you tell me going on here? I got a call that you had attacked somebody, Stacy Parks"

"What!! I did nothing. This woman here has a very active imagination and is making all sorts of unfounded accusations. I came for my appointment with Ms. Parks and I found her lying on the floor."

"What about the vase, what about the vase, you hit her on the head."

"I didn't hit anybody on the head, Roger knocked the vase over, I picked it up and I found Ms. Parks. And I really hope that somebody called a doctor because it's possible that this woman more than fainted. She might even be dead."

At that moment, Stacy Parks' personal doctor showed up. Fred and Jimmy both recognized him and Fred said, "Doc, can you see what state Ms. Parks is in??"

The secretary started to get hysterical again and was saying, she did it, she did it. Fred said, "Ok, that's enough out of you, Can you two," referring to the guards, "get her out of here. Actually one of you, you go take care of that arm, no doubt you had a run in with the cat." Fred gave a look at Roger, meanwhile Roger was as calm as could be, as though nothing had happened.

The doctor said, "Ms. Parks is dead, it appears to be a heart attack, but there is a bump in her head, I'm going to have to take her to my office to do a thorough examination. I will inform you of the results as soon as I have them."

Fred said, "No Doc, we gotta test the body for prints and do a complete examination of this room." Fred got on his radio and called the lab guys and said "come on down here, we have a possible murder I want to you examine this place from head to toe. Meanwhile, nobody leaves here until I say so, this whole place is on lockdown"

"Mandy, why does the secretary keep saying you did it?"

"Because when I found Stacy Parks, I was standing over the body with that vase, and she thinks I hit her over the head. I mean, Fred, I came to sign a contract to start a series of commercials with Roger."

Fred said, "No matter Mandy, you got come down to the station and make a statement and until we know more about this, you're also a suspect. Sorry Mandy, that's just the way it is. Not that I think you killed her, but I gotta do things by the book. You'll be able to go home, but right now, things are very murky."

Mandy said "You don't really think I killed her!!!???" She was beginning to freak out.

"No Mandy, but like I said, there are certain procedures that we have to go through and unfortunately, you gotta stay put and later we'll go to the station and you make a statement and then you can go home."

Mandy and Roger sat out in the reception area. The secretary was still beside herself with grief but was calmer. She heard something to the effect that Ms. Parks had a heart attack and started to realize that Mandy didn't kill

Ms. Parks. She was definitely the emotional type.

Amazingly, Roger just sat by Mandy and put his head on her lap. You wouldn't think this was the same cat that attacked the security guard before.

Mandy thought about making small talk with the secretary, but then thought against it, in case she started to think that somehow she was responsible for what happened to Ms. Parks. All she wanted was a chance to make some money, to maybe start something new in her life, and here she is, staring at another dead body through no fault of her own. She could think of all the years of her life, and other than her mother and husband, she had not had to face a dead body. And here it is, in the space of 3 weeks, she's had to face two, David Towsky and now Stacy Parks. Well, there goes that opportunity. But of all things, this really takes the dog biscuit.

After the lab guys performed all their tests, the doctor called an ambulance for the body. Two ambulance guys arrived with a stretcher and placed Ms. Parks carefully on it and took her out of the room. The way they were taking their time, they weren't trying to get anywhere in a hurry. There was nobody to save. That's how it is with all ambulance drivers. Once they know that the body is dead, they take it easy, fill out all the paper work and aren't going crazy trying to beat all the traffic. It's only when there's a chance of saving someone that they go all crazy with traffic and with their sirens. The sooner they get to the hospital, the more of a chance of the patient surviving.

At one point, the manager of Hedon Pet Nutrition, Carol Stamis arrived. She was a youngish brunette woman, in her late 20s who had that look of a business school graduate. Very well put together, attractive, but confident and all business at all times. A little later, the second party that arrived was Stacy Parks husband, Charles Parks. He was a man in his late 50s, early 60s, grey haired but also you could tell had been in business all his life, wore a suit, very well put together, neat hair and he still had most of his hair.

Charles Parks was asking a lot of questions, what had happened, when did this happen, was there a possibility of foul play or was it an accident and if it was foul play, what were the police going to do about this murder??? Fred said "We don't know yet for sure if it is a murder Mr. Parks, but we are taking this whole situation very seriously."

Just when Mandy thought that she couldn't take another 5 minutes of waiting in this place, Fred motioned to her that they could leave. Fred said "We'll take your car, I'll leave the police car for Jimmy, he's still filling in all the blanks and dealing with the various personalities."

Once in the car, Mandy started to tell Fred, "I tell you Fred, just yesterday I was speaking to her, and thinking that this was going to be a new money maker for me. I'm still out of a job, you know. I have absolutely no reason to kill Ms. Parks. If anything, I was looking forward to this relation because it meant that I would have money in the future. And now, she's dead. Hopefully of natural causes. Who knows if I'll get to make that commercial now. Luckily, I also got a call from another company, but they're smaller and they don't have the class of Hedon Foods, but the lady who runs it, Loretta Gumble, was certainly nice enough."

"You think she may have had cause to hurt Stacy Parks?"

"Nah, she was a small business owner, selling products and toys, not a competitor, just regular people. She even said, we're not as esoteric as Hedon. So, she knew the size of her business."

"While you were in the office, did you touch anything but the vase?"

"Nothing. The only reason I touched the vase was because of Roger knocking it over. At the time, I was just glad that it didn't break, but the vase is what led me to Stacy Parks laying there. If that hadn't happened, I may have just sat on a chair and kept wondering and asking myself, where is this woman?"

"You know Mandy, it's strange, before you had no contact with any murders, and since you solved the David Towsky case, here you are running into another dead body. Let's hope that it's not a murder, but a heart attack like the doc says.

"I know, I was just thinking that to myself before. I mean, you know me Fred, the last thing that I want is this kind of excitement. A great new job, a lot of tarot reading and zodiac charts, that's exciting. Dead people, not so exciting, actually it's pretty scary stuff. I thought I would never have to go through what happened to me with David, and here I am again in the middle of another strange death."

"Well, so far the Doctor is ruling it as a heart attack. He's going in the direction that she was alone in the office, she had a heart attack in the back of the room, secretary didn't hear her, and she fell down, and hit her head on something. Me, I'm always looking for the logical answer, not for the supernatural answer. The woman didn't have any enemies to speak of and certainly nobody that would kill her, she has run a pretty clean business, so there's no reason to suspect foul play. And there's no evidence to support that either."

"Yes, I remember from David."

"And you see, eventually you found evidence to the contrary. Whatever you do, don't get involved in this ok, let us handle it."

"Oh, believe me, I'm not touching this with a 10 foot pole. The situation with David was different he was my friend, and I didn't feel that his death was natural. However, I only talked to this woman yesterday, and saw her for the first time today, unfortunately dead. So, I have no interest whatsoever in any replays. The situation as far as I'm concerned is closed, if they call me back and want to do a commercial, fine, but meanwhile, I think I'm going to talk to the other woman. That sounds like a straight up situation where Roger is filmed and everybody goes home at the end of the day and we all live happily ever after.

"Even when I first dealt with Stacy Parks, she had me watch a company video about what they do and believe me, this is a VERY fancy operation. So, it's either a commercial with one company or the other.

"I'm glad to hear it Mandy, I just didn't want you to have any more problems. Anyway, once at the station, just give me a report and you can go home, I'm sure this was not the day you were planning."

"You got that right!!"

Thank You! If you've enjoyed "Murder at the Art Gallery", would you please take a minute to leave a review on Amazon. Even just a few sentences would be great. When you leave a review it helps others who are looking for new cozy mysteries to read, and it helps me improve the books. Plus I'd love to hear what you think.

Be sure to get your FREE audiobook of "Murder at the Art Gallery here:

http://audiobooksignup.higher-understanding.com.

You'll also be informed of when new books in the series are going to be released.

Thank you, Eleanor Kittering

ABOUT THE AUTHOR

In a world filled with cozy mystery writers, Eleanor Kittering saw that there was still one little nook that hadn't been filled, so, she's fulfilling that part of the female sleuth universe.

And in a world filled with all types of heroines, in this book we have one that never wanted to solve a mystery, but somehow winds up doing it, and who owns a cat that could help her but doesn't know that he can.

So please, check out how a zodiac, tarot reading housewife from New Jersey and her somewhat mystical cat find justice for the murder of her friend. .

Made in the USA
Middletown, DE
12 January 2020